U0125016

上海旅游实用指南

Practical Guide to Shanghai

（英文版）

Edited by

Shanghai Municipal Tourism Administrative Commission

Shanghai People's Fine Arts Publishing House

Please understand that if the information offered in this book will be changed as the sights of the city is developing continually.

Foreword

上海简介

Shanghai, also named "Hu" or "Shen" in short, is situated at 31°14' north latitude and 121°29' east longitude, the middle of China's east coastline. It occupies a total area of 6,341sq. km. (of which Pudong New Area occupies 523sq. km.), with a total resident population of over 17,000,000. It has a pleasant climate, with four distinct seasons. The average temperature is around 18°C and the annual rainfall is 1,240mm.

Shanghai, an open city on the coast famous for its history and culture, is a gate to the Yangtze River delta. It is a municipality under the direct jurisdiction of the Central Government, the largest economic and trade center, a comprehensive industrial base and the leading port in China.

Shanghai is well-known in the world not only for its prosperous cosmopolitan feature but also for its rich humanistic resources. In recent years, a number of modern buildings have been added to the city, such as the Oriental Pearl TV Tower, Shanghai Museum, Shanghai Library, Shanghai Stadium, Shanghai Grand Theatre, Shanghai Circus City, Shanghai Urban-Planning Exhibition Hall, Jin Mao Tower and Shanghai Science & Technology Museum. They have become new scenic sights in Shanghai. Colorful festivities, like Shanghai Tourism Festival and Shanghai International Art Festival, have attracted an increasing number of tourists from home and abroad.

Shanghai's tourist infrastructure is getting more and more accomplished. By the end of 2004, there were 40 international travel services, 700 domestic travel services and 350 star-rated hotels with about 65,000 rooms. Shanghai is an ideal "paradise" for shoppers. There are commercial streets and shopping areas like the famous Nanjing Pedestrian Road, Huaihai Road, North Sichuan Road, Yuyuan Commercial and Tourist Area, the Ever Bright Commercial City, Xujiahui Commercial Area and Zhangyang Road Commercial Area in Pudong. There, shops stand rows upon rows with large collections of beautiful commodities, meeting the needs of tourists of different levels. Shanghai is also a paradise for gourmets. There are over a thousand restaurants, serving the 16 different styles of food in China, such as Beijing, Sichuan, Guangdong, Yangzhou, Fujian, etc. There are Western restaurants serving French, Russian, Italian, English, German, Japanese and Indian food and also Muslim and vegetarian food. In Shanghai, one can have a taste of all the delicacies in the world. Shanghai is well developed in communications by land, water and air. There are over 40 Chinese and foreign air companies opening about 300 air routes dispatching from Shanghai. Shanghai Railway Station dispatches every day 80 lines of trains back and forth from Shanghai. Shanghai also boasts the Shanghai-Nanjing, Shanghai-Hangzhou-Ningbo Freeways, and the Pudong International Airport, whose annual passenger transport volume reaches 20,000,000 person/times. Plus that of the Hongqiao International Airport, it is over 30,000,000 person/times. Metro line No.1 and No.2 and the light-rail first phase project are in operation. Together with the 100 special tour bus lines connecting Shanghai with neighbouring tourist areas, they will render faster service and more convenience in urban communications to tourists. Recently, the maglev has also been opened to the public. It offers travelers a zero height of flight at 430 km/hr.

On Dec. 3, 2002, Shanghai succeeded in winning the bid for the sponsorship of World Expo 2010. The world has given China a share of luck and Shanghai will add more splendor to the world. Shanghai is ushering in excellent opportunities for development. People of Shanghai warmly welcome visitors from home and abroad.

CONTENTS 目录

观光车

Most popular attractions

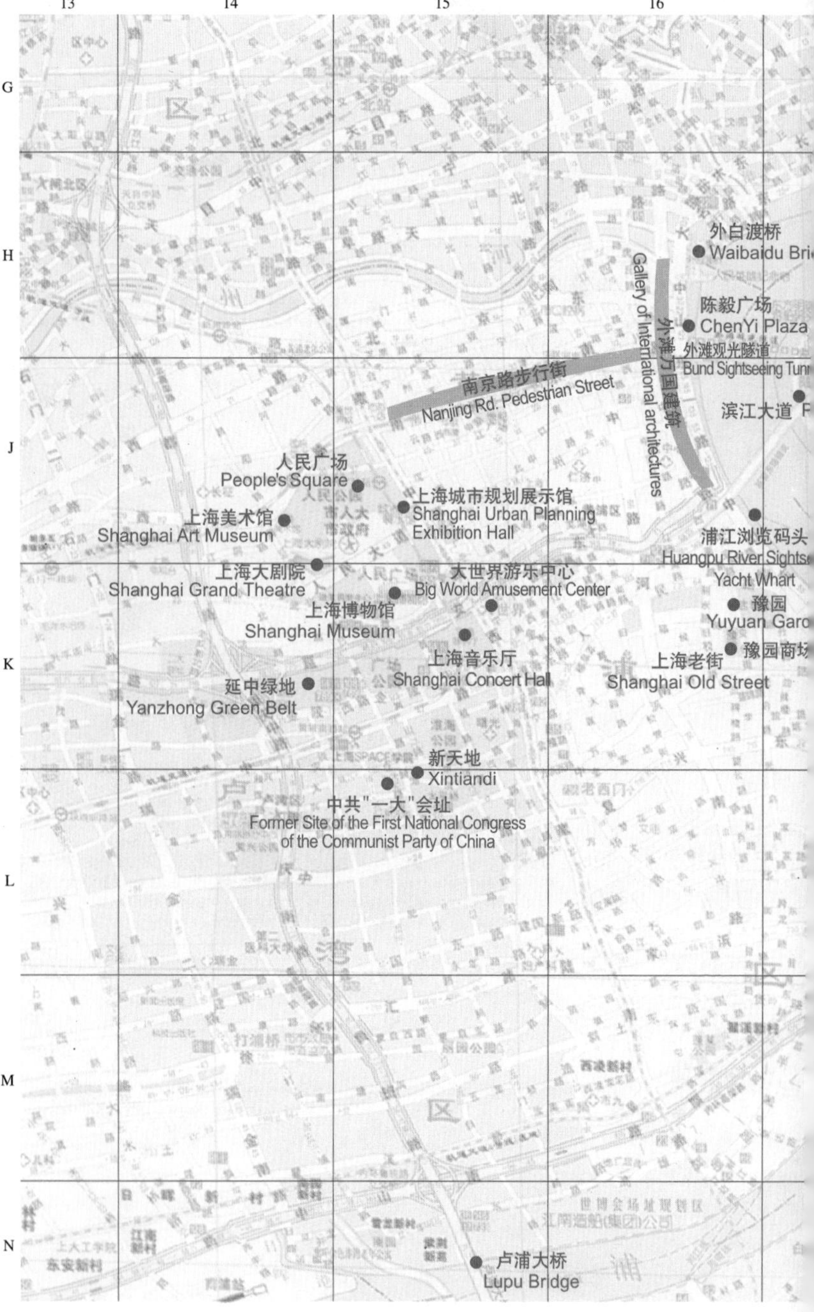

in central Shanghai 上海市中心最受欢迎景点

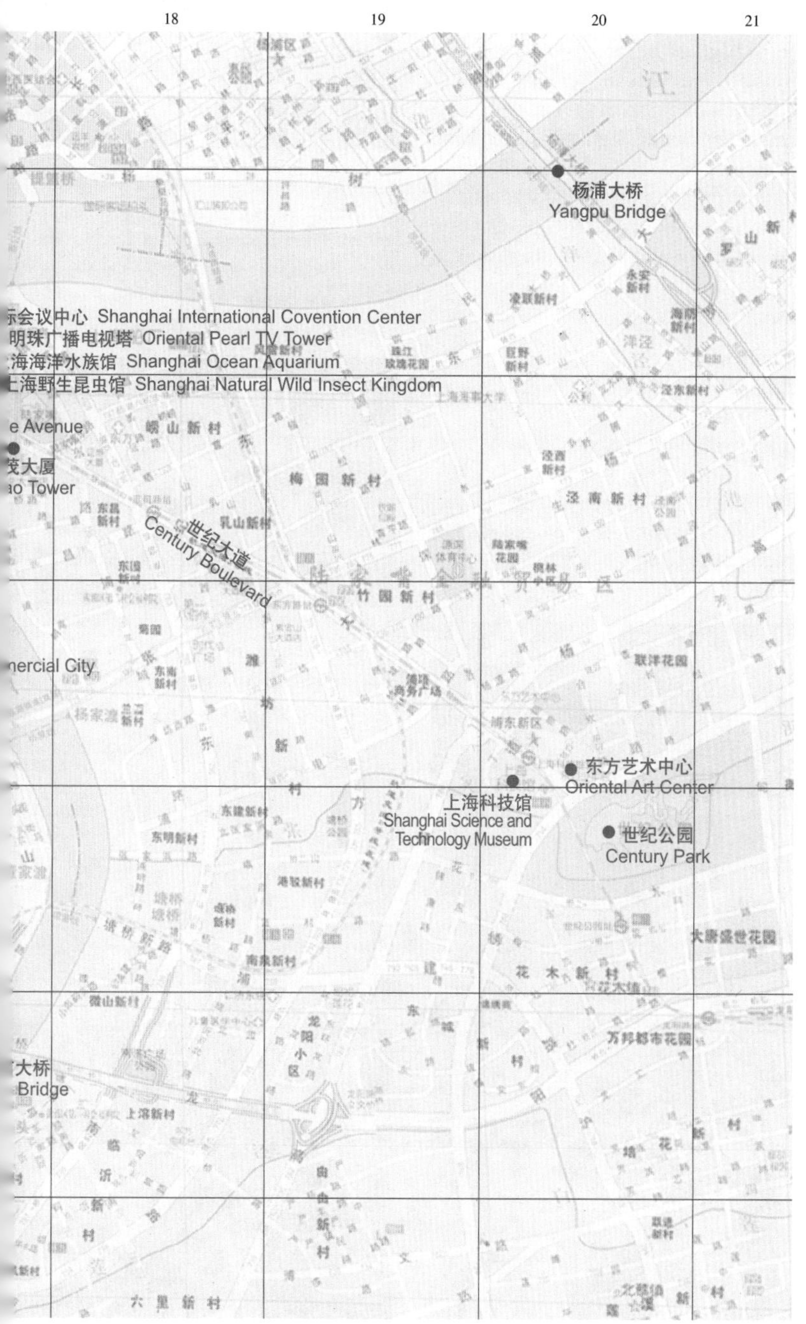

ORIENTAL PEARL TV TOWER H17

东方明珠广播电视塔

◆ The Oriental Pearl TV Tower, completed on Oct. 1, 1994, with a height of 468 m, is the highest in Asia and the third highest in the world, only next to the TV towers in Toronto, Canada and Moscow, Russia. It is an integrated center, combining sightseeing, catering, shopping, amusement, hotel accommodation, broadcasting and TV transmission into one entity. It is a symbolic architecture and tourist attraction in Shanghai.

- 8:30
- 21:30
- 50 yuan
- 021-58791888
- No. 1 Pudong Century Boulevard
  浦东世纪大道 1 号
- Metro Line No.2, public buses 81, 82, 85, 870, Bund sightseeing Tunnel, Ferryboat Taigong Line
- about 60 minutes

* The Revolving Restaurant, 267 m high from the ground, is the highest revolving restaurant in Asia. It can accommodate 300 diners at one time. Through the French windows in the restaurant one can have a 360° bird's-eye view of the scenery on both sides of the river.

* The dazzling spherical observation deck, 263-m-high, with a dia. of 45m, is an ideal place for having a bird's-eye view of the city.

* The towering space cabin, 350-m-high, consists of an observation deck, a conference hall and a cafe.

* The lower sphere in the tower contains an outdoor sightseeing corridor and the Museum of Shanghai Historical Development.

* Shanghai Historical Development Exhibition Hall, located inside the TV Tower, with an exhibition area of 10,000 sq.m. The museum consists of 7 parts: The Origin of Huating (ancient Shanghai); Features of the Urban City; Glimpses of the Open Port; a 10-mile Street of Foreign Flavor; Traces on the Sea; an Exposition of Architecture; and Good Times of Cars and Carriages. There are over 1,000 exhibits of precious cultural relics for spectators to appreciate history and culture while being entertained by a dis-play of innovative concepts.

The museum adopts the display with "real objects in the scenes" supplemented with hi-tech methods, combining cultural relics, stage properties, models, sound and light into one. The exhibition demonstrates to visitors the way of life and work in old Shanghai and the folk customs and habits of old Shanghai citizens.

* Oriental Pearl TV Tower yacht wharf is located on the banks of Huangpu River, covering an area of over 2,200 sq.m. Visitors can take a yacht to have a cruise on the Huangpu River and to appreciate the flourishing urban scene.

JINMAO TOWER J17

金茂大厦

◆ Jinmao Tower is one of the buildings that symbolize Shanghai's marching toward the 21st century. Its height, 420.5 m, is next to the Double Tower in Kuala Lumpur in Malaysia and the Sears Building in Chicago, USA. It boasts the highest in China and the third highest in the world.

- 8:30
- 21:00
- 50 yuan (jin mao observatory 88)
- 021-50476688
- No. 88 Pudong Century Boulevard 浦东世纪大道 88 号
- Tour bus No 3, Metro line No.2 (Lujiazui Station) public buses 81, 82, 870, 871, 872, Tunnel lines 3, 4, 5 and 6
- about 30 minutes

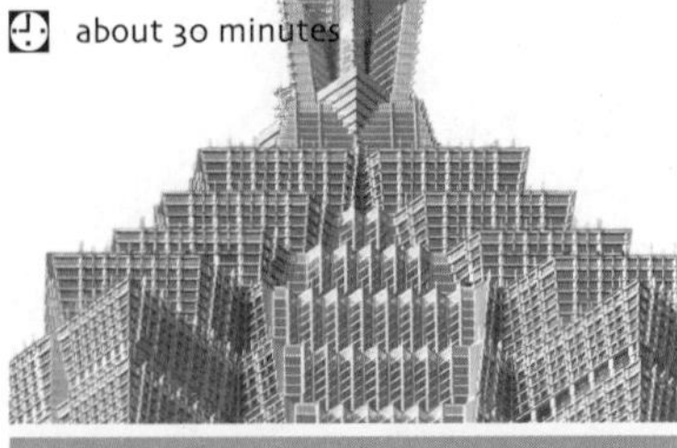

* On floors 3-50 are spacious, bright and pillarless offices, able to accommodate 10,000 office workers at one time.

* Floors 53-87 belong to five-star Jinmao Grand Hyatt Hotel, the highest hotel in the world.

* The cylindrical floors 56 to the top, 142m high and 27 in dia., is the "atrium in the air". Sunlight is refracted through the glass. Surrounding the atrium are 555 guest rooms of different sizes and styles, and different Chinese and Western restaurants.

* On the 87 floor is the restaurant in the air.

* The observation deck on the 88 floor, 341m high from the ground, is the highest in the country for sightseeing. It can accommodate over 1,000 visitors at one time. Two high-speed elevators at 9.1m/sec. transport visitors to the observation deck from the basement in 45 seconds.

SHANGHAI INTERNATIONAL CONVENTION CENTER H17

上海国际会议中心

◆ Shanghai International Convention Center, located on Pudong Riverside Avenue, together with the Oriental Pearl TV Tower, forms a scenic sight in Lujiazui area. It has a floor space of 110,000 sq.m. Oriental Riverside Hotel is a five-star hotel integrating catering,conference and exhibition, tourism and recreation, whose unique shape has made it one of ten classic architectures in Shanghai since New China was founded. Many well-known international conferences have been held here, such as 99 'Fortune' Global Forum, 2001 APEC Leaders Summit, the 35th Asia Development Bank Annual Meeting, and the Fifth APEC Ministerial Meeting on Telecommunications and Informtation Industry.

- 8:30
- 16:30
- 50 yuan (only for group reservation)
- 021-50370000
- No. 2727 Riverside Avenue, Pudong 浦东滨江大道2727号
- Tour bus No.3, Metro line No.2 (Lujiazui Station) public buses 81, 82, 870, 871, 872, Tunnel lines 3, 4, 5 and 6
- 30 minutes

* In the modernized conference hall, there are 4,300-sq.m. modernized multi-functional halls and a 3,600- sq.m. news center.

* Luxurious guest rooms: The hotel consists of 270 guest rooms, including presidential suites, standard suites, executive suites and business suites overlooking the river.

* First-class catering: These are various Chinese and western restaurants such as riverside hall, Shanghai restaurant, European resaurant, Asia restaurant, Star and Moon Cafe, etc. Shanghai restaurant, is the largest multifunctional pil-lar-less banquet hall in China, capable of holding 3,000 people.

* Recreation Services: The center provides complete recreation services such as a ball room, a gym, a swimming pool, a bowling room, a bill-iard room, mini golf course, a sauna room, pingpong room, massage room and a shopping arcade.

PUDONG RIVERSIDE AVENUE J17

浦东滨江大道

◆ Pudong Riverside Avenue runs from Dongchang Road Wharf in the south to Taitongzhan Wharf in the north, with a total length of 2.5 km. The avenue consists of the embankment, the riverside road, the touching-water platform, the musical fountain and the yacht wharf, forming a "New Bund" in Pudong.

- 8:00
- 23:00
- 021-58875487
- No. 700 Lujiazui Rd., Pudong
  陆家嘴路 700 号
- Tour bus No. 3, Metro Line No. 2 (Lujiazui Station) public buses 81, 82, 870, 871, 872, Tunnel lines 3, 4, 5 and 6

* The Riverside Acenue was designed in three-dimensional layout. The green belt, flower bed, fountain and sculptures look unique and beautiful. The waterside platform, greening slope, half-sinking area and sightseeing avenue combine to form a sightseeing corridor.

* There is a lake, a waterside pavilion, a six-cornered pavilion, little bridges, rockeries, landscaped corridors amidst tall trees and florescent bushes, forming a scene of a classical garden, offering visitors with an environment of peace and tranquility, and helping them escape the metropolitan hubbubs.

* Pudong Riverside Avenue has become a favorite scenic spot and recreational spot in Shanghai.

SHANGHAI OCEAN AQUARIUM H17

上海海洋水族馆

◆ Located in Pudong Lujiazui Area Shanghai Ocean Aquarium is a newly built hi-tech tourist establishment. It occupies an area of 22,000 sq.m. with a 155-m-long seabed observation tunnel, boasting the longest in Asia. Visitors will find themselves at the bottom of the sea and can appreciate the wonderful and mysterious creatures in the sea world.

The aquarium is divided into 9 sections with 32 large theme creature exhibition areas displaying over 15,000 rare fishes of 350 species from the four continents and the five oceans, including precious species from fresh water and sea water and rare species from different places in China. The aquarium enables visitors to have a wonderful experience of traveling to the five continents through the water world.

- 9:00
- 21:00
- 110 yuan (adults), 70 yuan (children)
- 021-58779988
- No. 158 Yincheng Rd. (N), Lujiazui 陆家嘴银城北路158号
- Tour bus 3 Metro line No.2 (Lujiazui Station), public buses 85, 81 and 82
- about 60 minutes

* The "mosts" in the aquarium

The only aquarium in China that has "Chinese exhibition area"

The only place in the world where leaf sea otter and grass sea otter can live in one tank.

It is the aquarium where sea horse and aeoliscus strigatus lived the longest.

The largest Malapterurus electricus exhibited in Asia.

The only aquarium in the world which has 6 grass carps.

The only observation tunnel where amazon tropical rain forest are exhibited.

The most successful project of shark egg development in China.

It is where the only one and the most expensive jellyfish in China is exhibited.

The only pair of Pristis cuspidtus in China.

The aquarium has the most species of sea animals in China (over 320 species).

The aquarium has the most tiger sharks in one tank.

It has the only tank in which one can appreciate the seals swimming under water.

SHANGHAI NATURAL WILD INSECT KINGDOM H17

上海野生昆虫馆

◆ Shanghai Natural Wild Insect Kingdom, located between the Riverside Avenue and the Oriental Pearl TV Tower, is the first of its kind in China, serving as a center for tourism, appreciation and scientific education.

Walking into the museum, you will find yourself amidst a rural scenery. There are insect species from different ecological environments of water, desert, rain forest, islands, and marshes. You will experience the miraculous charm of nature.

- 9:00 (winter) 17:00
- 9:00 (summer) 21:00
- 35 yuan (20 yuan for children)
- 021-58406950
- No.1 Fenghe Rd. 丰和路1号
- Tour bus 3, Metro line No.2 (Lujiazui Station), Public buses 85, 81, 82
- 60minutes

✻ The museum is divided into the Insect Corridor, Valley of Butterflies, Caves of Amphibious Reptiles, Ecological Touching Area, Tropical Rain Forest, Desert Dragon and Scientific Education Classroom.

✻ The most distinctive feature of the museum is that visitors are allowed to touch and feel many lively creatures, feed animals, watch animal show and make specimens, enjoying the pleasure given by Mother Nature.

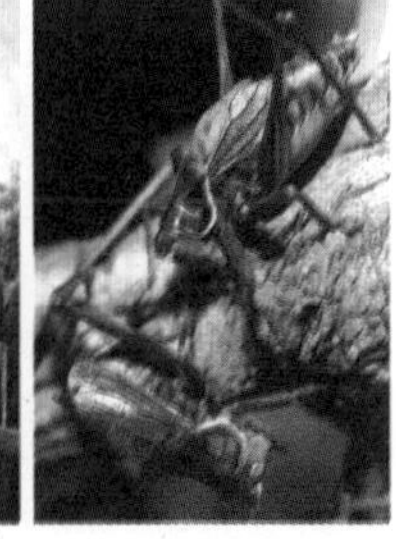

LUJIAZUI CENTRAL GREEN SPACE J17

陆家嘴中心绿地

◆ The 10-hectare green belt, at the exit of Yan'an Road (E) Tunnel and in the heart of Lujiazui Finance Zone, is the largest green belt open free to the public. The undulating topography is mainly covered with lawns, dotted by lakes, designed in simple and natural style, forming a pleasant and attractive scenic spot that can be called "a green lung in the metropolis".

- 8:30
- 22:00
- 021-58875487
- No. 160 Lujiazui Rd., Pudong 浦东陆家嘴路160号
- Tour bus No. 3, Metro Line No.2 (Lujiazui Station) Public buses 81, 82, 85
- about 30 minutes

✻ The lawn in Lujiazui Green Space occupies an area of 6.5 hectares. The grass is an evergreen, cold-season species imported from Europe.

✻ In the middle of the lawn are planted willows, magnolias, gingkoes, camphor trees, pines, maples, metasequoia, boxes, presenting a scene of vigor and vitality.

* At the entrance there is a sculpture with "spring" as its theme—composed of 8 steel "flowers". In the middle of the lake is the main fountain surrounded by double-coiled fountains that looks like a dragon soaring to the sky. By the side of the lake is a 28-m high tent for visitors to enjoy the view.

* The zigzag paths on the lawns form the picture of a magnolia, the city flower of Shanghai. In the middle of the magnolia design is a 8,600-sq. m. lake in the shape of the map of Pudong.

SHANGHAI SCIENCE AND TECHNOLOGY MUSEUM K20

上海科技馆

◆ Located in Pudong Huamu Administrative and Cultural Center and near the Century Boulevard and the Century Park, Shanghai Science and Technology Museum occupies a floor area of 98,000 sq. m. With "Nature, Man and Science and Technology" as its theme, it is an important base for science popularization and technology, as well as leisure and tourism. With investment from Shanghai municipal government, it is the first large project of society and culture launched to improve the public's science knowledge. APEC informal summit 2001 was held here.

- 9:00 (close on Mondays)
- 17:00 (ticket hour: 8:45—15:30)
- 60 yuan (adult) 45 yuan (student)
- 021-68542000
- No. 2000 Century Boulevard
  世纪大道2000号
- Metro Line No.2 (Shanghai Science and Technology Museum Station), public buses 794, 640 and 983
- about 60 minutes

* In the museum there are exhibition areas of different styles, three theaters: IMAX 3-D theater, IMAX 3-D Dome Theatre, 4-D theatre, and facilities like tourism souvenir stores, a temporary exhibition hall, a multi-functional hall and a bank.

* The Central Hall in the middle of the museum occupies an area of 1,480 sq.m. A spheroid in the shape of an egg yolk standing in the oblong lobby symbolizes the pregnancy of life and implies the unlimited expanse of the universe, the magnitude of history and earth-shaking achievement of modern science and technology.

* The exhibition areas on 1st floor

The Spectrum of Life—In tropical rain forests, stone forests and Dai bamboo house, the diversity of species, ecology and genes is shown.

The "Earth Explorations"—Maglev earth, rock corridor, crust story, volcanic eruption and earthquake reveal the mystery of the crust.

Audio Visual Paradise—you can experience the glamour of modern audio-visual technology.

Children's Technological Garden—a key to open children's mind, it fosters children's intelligence as well as allows children to feel the charm of nature.

Light of Wisdom—you can experience happiness in participating and learn basic technologies while enjoying yourself.

Cradle of the Designer—Everybody could be an excellent designer, with the assistance of CAD technology.

* Exhibition areas on 2nd floor

Earth Home—earth, is the home to humankind. Earth Exploration here provokes our reflections on earth's sustainable development.

Information Era—You will experience the information period through participating hi-tech programs.

Robots' World—the versatile robots give a wonderful performance displaying the development of modern robot technology.

* Exhibition areas on the 3rd floor

Light of Exploration—what you can see here are the major techlogical achievements in the 20th century and a historical explorations of scientists in the past.

Human and Health—Tips to live a healthier life.

Astonomical World—Get to know all the science and technologies used in human's voyage to the sky.

* Science Popularization Corridor:

Technologies in Ancient China—The glorious technological achievements in ancient China is showed artistically.

(1st floor)

* 4-D theatre—Capable of holding 56 visitors it is a bold use of Disney concept on theaters. The fountain, wind, smoke and three-dimensional film combine to bring the visitors a brand-new experience.

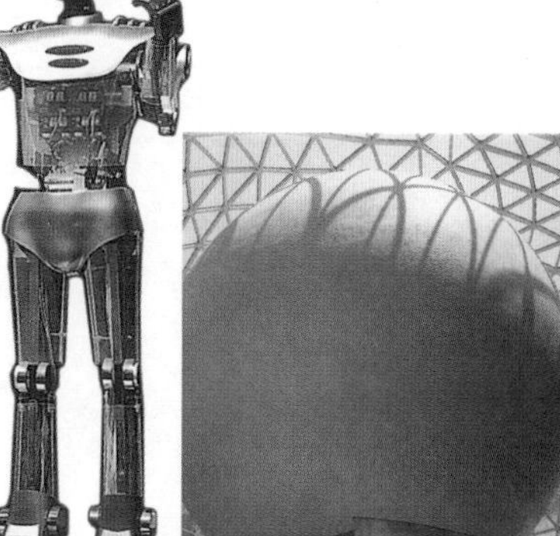

CENTURY BOULEVARD J18

世纪大道

◆ Designed by a French company, Century Boulevard is full of French romance and famed as the "Avenue des Champs Elysees in the Orient". It boasts 8 Chinese botanical gardens such as the willow garden, cherry garden and magnolia garden, with hundreds of plants, which originated in China and now spread worldwide. Modern style lamps, fences, white shades, sundials, and time pillars accompany the avenue all the way. Roaming along the 5-kilometre-long road, tourists will appreciate its beautiful scenery.

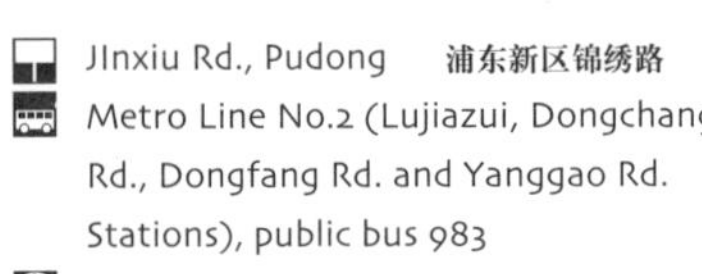

JInxiu Rd., Pudong 浦东新区锦绣路

Metro Line No.2 (Lujiazui, Dongchang Rd., Dongfang Rd. and Yanggao Rd. Stations), public bus 983

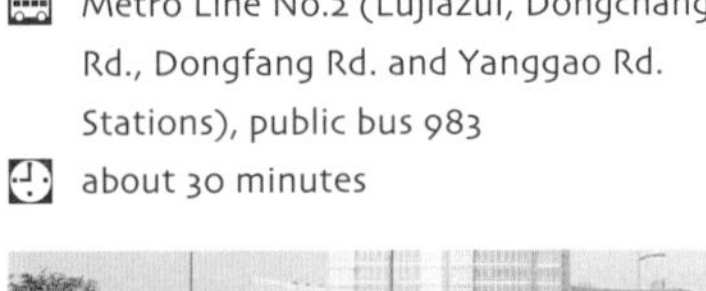

about 30 minutes

* Arranged unsymmetrically, the traffic lane of the road is 3-m-wide, the sidewalk on the north is 44.5-m-wide while the one on the south is 24.5-m-wide.

* The grand avenue is guarded by 6 rows of trees and 8 botanical gardens. It is a beautifully landscaped street.

CENTURY PARK L20

世纪公园

The Century Park in Pudong is at the end of the axial thoroughfare in Huamu Branch District with the Administrative and Cultural Center, Shanghai Science and Technology Museum and Pudong New Area Administrative Commission building on its north. On either end of the park is the Century Park stop and Yanggao Road station of metro line 2.

The park is designed to cover an area of 140.3 hectares with a total investment of RMB 844 million. It will be completed in two phases: the first phase covers an area of about 100 hectares. The planning of the park is an integration of the Eastern and Western cultures, of man and nature. It is a typical Chinese park with modern characteristics. The park mainly consists of large plots of lawns, woods and lakes. There are such scenic spots as the Central Lake Island, the Meeting Square, the Native Pastoral, and the International Garden, accompanied by facilities for protection of birds, experience of science, open air performances and children's playground.

- 7:00
- 18:00
- 10 yuan
- 021-38760588
- No. 1001 Jinxiu Rd., Pudong
  浦东锦绣路 1001 号
- Metro line No.2, public buses 788, 794, long-distance buses She-Bao line, Nan-Yang line and Shen-San line
- about 60 minutes

PEOPLE'S SQUARE J15

人民广场

◆ Located in downtown Shanghai with an area of about 140,000 sq.m., it is the largest public square in Shanghai. Since the 1990s, it has been renovated several times. In the northern end of the square is the Municipal City Hall; in the southern end is Shanghai Museum. Shanghai Grand Theatre, another symbolic cultural building in Shanghai, is on the northwest and Shanghai Urban Planning Exhibition Hall on the northeast stand facing each other in the distance. The now square is Shanghai's political and cultural center, as well as a new scenic spot.

People's Avenue
人民大道

Tour bus 10, Metro Line No.1 and No.2 (People's Square Station), public buses 17, 18, 20, 23, 37, 49, 123, 926, Tunnel lines 3 and 6

about 60 minutes

* Under the square is People's Sqare Station of Metro Line No.1 linking two modern malls—Hong Kong Famous Brand Street and Dimei Underground Mall.

* The People's Avenue, 600-m-long and 32-m- wide, paved with granite, runs in front of the City Hall. On each side of the avenue there is a 5.5-m-wide partition green belt and a 6.5-m-wide lane for unmotorized vehicles.

* On the southern side of the avenue are three underground buildings: a multi function underground mall, a city underground transformer house, the largest in Asia, and a 20,000-sq.m. underground parking lot which boasts the largest in Shanghai.

⁕ In the middle of the square there is a 320-sq.m. circular fountain. The center of the fountain is the map of Shanghai, surrounded by three layers of fountains, fitted with lights. When the fountain ejects, the water column reaches a height of 20 m. When it stops ejecting, tourists can go inside. There are three flights of steps, each fitted with colored glass and lit from beneath. When lights are on, at night there are the three colored halos of red, yellow and blue. The circumference of the fountain is carved out of whole blocks of granite and fitted with drum-shaped lamps.

⁕ Dotted with trees and flower-beds, the large tract of 80,000 sq.m. lawn, together with the fountain, the sculptures, artistic lantern pillars, stone chairs and stools form a picturesque scenery.

⁕ Over 1,000 pigeons in the western corner of the square bring peace and tranquility to people and form a delightful cultural scene. On festival days and holidays, the avenue is always bustling with crowds of visitors.

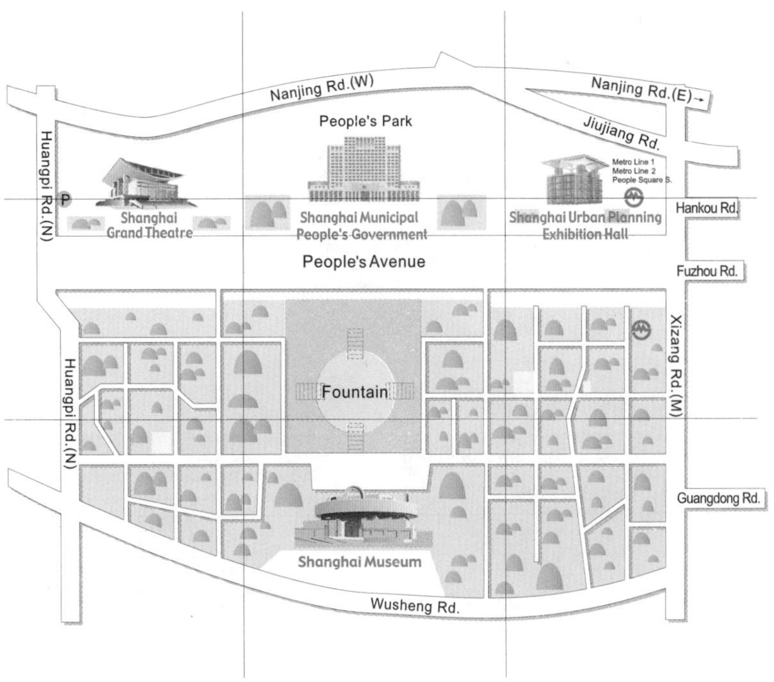

SHANGHAI GRAND THEATRE J14

上海大剧院

◆ With a floor area of 70,000 sq.m., and a height of 40m, Shanghai Grand Theatre in the People's Square next to the City Hall was built with a total investment of US 60 million. It was designed by a French architect in a unique style, integrating the flavor of Chinese culture with that of the Western. It provides a stage for world-class operas, dances, films and concerts. It is a symbolic building of culture in Shanghai.

- 8:00-11:00
- 13:00-16:00
- 40 yuan (adult), 30 yuan(student)
- 021-63868686
- No. 190 Huangpi Rd. (N)
  黄陂北路 190 号
- Metro Line No.2 (People Square Station), public buses 18, 46, 49, 71, 127, 145 and Tunnel line 6
- about 40 minutes

* The white arc roof and the light reflecting transparent glass walls together ingeniously form into a crytal palace.

* In the theatre there are a 550-seat medium-sized theatre and a 250-seat small theatre, available for performance of chamber music and song and dance drama.

* The stage in the main theatre is the largest of international standard, equipped with the most up-to-date stage changing facilities, able to accommodate the performances of world-grade ballets, operas and symphony orchestras. The auditorium has a seating capacity of 1,800 spectators.

SHANGHAI URBAN PLANNING EXHIBITION HALL J15

上海城市规划展示馆

◆ Shanghai Urban Planning Exhibition Hall has "city, man, environment, and development" as its theme, with an area of 4,000 sq.m., a height of 43.3m, a total floor area of 18,393 sq.m., and an exhibition area of 7,000 sq.m. on its four floors. On display are the overall planning of the city and major achievements of construction in Shanghai arranged with hi-tech methods.

There are totally five exhibition halls, a video conference center and a custom street. The lobby is also the "introductory hall", whose name is "the historical monument". In the interlayer is the "hall of historically and culturally famous city", where the modern Shanghai history is demonstrated. On the second floor is the "hall of urban planning and construction achieve-ments", where the construction achievements in the 50 years of Shanghai, especially the ones in the 1990s, are on display. On the third and fourth floor there is the "overall urban planning hall", where the Shanghai's overall planning in the forthcoming 20 years is exhibited.

9:00
17:00 (stop checking tickets at 16:00)
25 yuan
021-63184477
No. 100 People's Avenue
人民大道100号
Metro Line No.1 (People Square Station), public buses 18, 46, 49, 71, 127, 145 and Tunnel line 6, Tour line 10
about 60 minutes

＊ Lobby—The artistic model of "Shanghai morning" has integrated the Shanghai landmark architectures in all periods.

The second floor—Hall of urban planning and construction achievements

The interlayer—The ups and downs of Shanghai are displayed here, with numerous precious old photos revealing the rich and profound history and culture of Shanghai urban development.

The third floor—With the model of the city's core areas as its center, the landscape of Shanghai (within inner ring areas) as planned before the year 2020 is displayed with integrated technology of sound, light and electricity. The over 600-sq. m. model is the largest one of its kind in the world.

The fourth floor—What's emphasized here are the professional planning projects of Shanghai's future development, including short-term and long-term planning projects, the planning of deep water port, air hub, information hub, Huangpu River development, etc. They are displayed in exhibition sections of environment protection, greening, housing and tourism.

Basement 1—With the unique architectures in Shanghai in the 1930s, visitors can appreciate the typical Shikumen lanes, and architectures in the style of typical French, British and Japanese. Every architecture displayed here has a prototype.

SHANGHAI MUSEUM K15

上海博物馆

◆ The museum on the south of People's Square is one of Shanghai's new symbolic buildings. It has a collection of over 120,000 pieces of cultural relics displayed over a floor space of 12,000 sq.m. in 10 exhibition halls of the bronzes, pottery and porcelain, sculpture, calligraphy, paintings, seals, jade-ware, coins, furniture and arts and crafts of the national ethnic groups. It gives a complete picture of the brilliant history of China's ancient art.

- 9:00
- 17:00
- 20 yuan (5 yuan for students)
- 021-63723500
- No. 201 People's Avenue 人民大道 201 号
- Metro Line No.1 (People Square Station), public buses 18, 46, 49, 71, 127, 22, 505 and Tunnel line 6
- about 90 minutes

* Hall of Ancient Chinese Sculpture: The exhibits on display date from the Warring States to the Ming Dynasty, presenting the creative characteristics of the different ages. There are the simple and abstract colored wooden figurines of the Warring States and the graceful, true-to-life lady figurines of the Tang Dynasty. The exhibits present the different traditional folk styles of the sculptural art. The most attractive part is the sculptural art of Chinese Buddha statues, in graceful posture and lively charm.

* Hall of Chinese Ancient Bronze-ware: The bronze-ware on display are precious pieces, with unique modeling, exquisite decorative lines, historical records, beautiful epigraph, and excellent casting technique. There are the giant Dake tripod of the Western Zhou Dynasty, the Xi Zun (wine vessel) of late Spring and Autumn Period. Both of which are rare.

* Hall of Chinese Paintings of Different Dynasties: There are over 120 pieces of original Chinese paintings of the different dynasties. The paintings of the Tang Dynasty are smooth in lines and dark in colors, lively in figure and charm. Paintings developed in a variety of styles and technique during the Five Dynasties and Song Dynasty, while emphasizing on painting realistically, created fine brushwork with heavy colors, freehand brushwork with ink and splash ink. The scholars' paintings rising in the Song Dynasty

and developed in the Yuan, Ming and Qing Dynasties have formed the main stream in the Chinese painting circle. In the Ming Dynasty the different schools of Zhejiang, Suzhou, Songjiang, Yangzhou and Shanghai represent the painting achievements of the different periods. They also indicate the long tradition and rich contents of the Chinese painting.

* Hall of Chinese Calligraphy of Different Dynasties: As the new achievement of Shanghai Museum, it is a hall exclusively displaying over 80 pieces of calligraphy masterpieces, especially by famous calligraphers in the dynasties after the Tang and Song Dynasties.

* Hall of Chinese Ancient Jade-ware: Over 400 pieces of precious jade-ware of different Chinese dynasties are displayed in this hall which occupies an area of over 500 sq.m. A modern light-conducted fiber technique and a special base-stand are adopted for the exhibits, producing a glistening and exquisite effect on the beautiful carvings on the jade. There are exhibits like jade bird of Shang Dynasty, and jade Sheng with Siling pattern in East Han Dynasty.

* Hall of Chinese Coins of Different Dynasties: The museum enjoys a reputation for the quality and amount of collection of coins. In the 730-sq.m. hall, nearly 7,000 pieces range from the Qin Dynasty down to the Ming and Qing Dynasties displayed in 7 parts, giving a description of the history and development of Chinese currencies in circulation and the economic and cultural exchanges with foreign countries.

* Hall of Arts and Crafts of Chinese Ethnic Groups: On display are costumes, embroideries, carvings,metal wares, pottery and lacquer ware, and painted masks of Chinese ethnic groups of unique style and color variety. They reflect the life-style and the pursuit for beauty of the different ethnic groups in China.

* Hall of Chinese Furniture of the Ming and Qing Dynasties: It consists of 5 parts, displaying over 100 pieces of Ming and Qing dynasty furniture. There are the simply designed and stream-line shaped Ming Dynasty furniture and the Qing Dynasty large and heavy ones. There are the reproductions of the scenes of the living rooms and studies. Those furnitures on display has aroused strong interests of cultural relic fans at home and abroad.

* Hall of Ancient Chinese Pottery and Porcelain: It is one of the museum's special exhibitions, and blends the Chinese ceramic history, arts appreciation with artissearch. Here we can see the colored pottery, the primitive blue porcelain and the colored, glazed pottery. Some of them are rare pieces in the world, and are exhibited for the first time.

SHANGHAI ART MUSEUM J14

上海美术馆

◆ Located at No.325 Nanjing Road (W), it is a museum equipped with modern facilities and multi-functions of modern cultural standard.

The 4-storied main building occupies an area of 2,200 sq.m., with a floor area of 5,977 sq.m. and a beautiful shape. The main gate faces the east. The semi-circular screen wall is made of dark brown glass supported by an aluminum-alloy frame. The side walls are inlaid with polished granite surface. The interior of the museum is fitted with modern devices that control temperature, humidity and light, and with fire-prevention, theft and damage guarding alarm. It is the most modernized museum in China.

- 9:00
- 17:00 (stop entering at 16:00)
- 20 yuan (5 yuan for students)
- 021-63270827
- No. 325 Nanjing Rd. (W)
  南京西路 325 号
- Metro Line No.1, No.2 (People Square Station) Public buses 20, 37 and 23
- about 60 minutes

* The museum collects around 3,000 masterpieces of fine arts. Some are works by famous artists in the country and some by founders of the Shanghai school paintings. There are also works by Hong Kong, Macao and Taiwan artists and overseas master painters. The vast art fans embrace these exhibitions which are irregularly displayed.

* Since its founding in 1956 the gallery has sponsored 1,226 domestic and overseas exhibitions of fine arts, calligraphy and photography. There were exhibitions of fine works from the United States, Canada, Britain, France, Italy, Denmark, Switzerland, Spain, Korea and Japan. The number of visitors in a year ranges from more than 300,000 to over 1,300,000.

SHANGHAI MAGLEV TRAIN

磁悬浮列车

Shanghai Maglev train, the first commercial maglev in the world, starts from Longyang Road station of Metro Line No.2, to Pudong International Airport, running a total length of 30 kilometres. The highest speed is 431 kilometres per hour. It takes 7 minutes and 20 seconds for a single trip.

This cutest train in the world has a railway engine of 27.196 metres in length and 3.7 metres in width, and carriages of 24.768 meters long. It only takes 14 minutes for a return trip. You will have wonderful experience in this "airplane on land".

* With their air ticket of that day, all passengers can buy a single-trip ticket of Maglev at a discount of 20% percentage off, namely, 40 yuan for ordinary seats and 80 yuan for VIP seats.

With their Maglev tickets, all passengers can pay a free visit to the Maglev Technology Exhibition Hall, located on the first floor of Longyang Road Maglev Station.

7:00

21:00 (the bus departs every 15 minutes)

single 50 yuan, return 80 yuan (ordinary)
single 100 yuan, return 160 yuan (VIP)

021-28907777

Maglev Longyang Rd. Station:
No. 2100 Longyang Rd. 龙阳路站—浦东机场
Maglev Pudong International Airport Station:
east of terminal building in Shanghai Pudong International Airport (directly linked by a 300-metre-long corridor)

Metro Line No.2, public buses 983, 976, bridge line 5 or 6, Shenjiang line

about 15 minutes

SHANGHAI CONCERT HALL K15

上海音乐厅

Shanghai Concert Hall was founded in 1930 in a traditional European style which was rarely seen in Shanghai.

Upon entering the lobby, you will see 16 majestic brown marble pillars.

The audience hall is of standard, explicit, complicated yet well-ordered layout, of light and solemn hue, which is in amazing harmony with the symphony performed there. The high-quality acoustic equipment has been approved by artists at home and abroad.

There are totally 1,122 seats in the concert hall, and the stage is 8.35 m. in depth, and 16 m. in width. It is about 100 sq.m..

Various well-renowned artists have performed here and gained huge success, including violinists Stern, Accardo, Zukerman, Pianists Laluozha, Fu Cong, Yin Chengzhong, Philadelpia Symphony Orchestra, Hongkong Philarmonic Orchestra, and China Symphony Orchestra.

021-63869153

西藏中路、金陵中路路口

public buses 02, 17, 18, 123, 112, Metro Line No.1 and No.2

NANJING ROAD PEDESTRIAN STREET J15

南京路步行街

◆ Nanjing Road, famed as "No.1 Street in China", is an epitome of Shanghai's history and culture. The 1,033-m-long Pedestrian Street lies between the Bund and the People's Square. There are more than 600 shops dotted on both sides of the street, such as the 100-year old ones, famous-brand ones and specialty shops of different trades. It is a most complete display of the varieties and brands of commodities in China, even in southeast Asia, meeting the needs of different consumers.

人民广场地铁站（南京路步行街）出口

Metro Line No.1 (People's Square Station), No.2 (People's Sqaure Station, Henan Rd.(M) Station) public buses 20, 37, 921, 18, 17, 22, 55, 21 and 23

Nanjing Road in the old days

* The street is open to the public round the clock. Several hundred thousands of visitors from all places in China and the world come here for sightseeing, shopping or just taking a walk to have some experience of the life-style of the metropolis. The crowd is only another landscape.

茂昌眼鏡公司
上海市第一食品商店
西服专卖

WORLD ARCHITECTURE AT THE BUND J16
外滩万国建筑

◆ The Bund is a symbol of Shanghai. The buildings are harmonious in color and style, thus gaining the name of "gallery of international architectures". There are the Gothic pointed roofs, ancient Greek vaults, Baroque columns and Spanish balconies. When night falls and the lights are on, all the buildings are lit with colorful lights, glistening and dazzling to the eye.

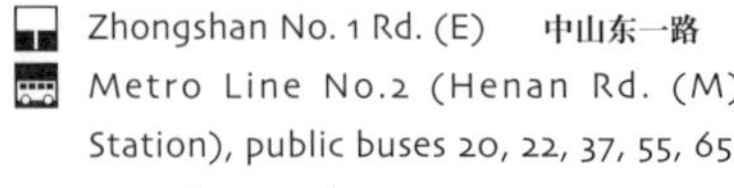

Zhongshan No. 1 Rd. (E) 中山东一路
Metro Line No.2 (Henan Rd. (M) Station), public buses 20, 22, 37, 55, 65, 42, 126, 135 and 145
about 60 minutes

The Bund in the old days

✻ 1-Shanghai Mansion
Built in 1934 on No. 20 Nothern Suzhou Rd.
And designed by a British real estate company, the "X-shaped", 22-storied Shanghai Mansion (formerly known as the Broadway Mansion) was an apartment complex for senior employees of British and Shanghai Commercial Bank, covering an area of 2,917 sq.m., and a floor area of 24,596 sq.m., The complex looks simple and clear, yet still gorgeous. It has been converted into a hotel since 1951.

✻ 2-Bank of China
Build in 1936
No. 23 Zhongshan Rd. (E1)
Designed by Lu Qianshou and Gonghe foreign firm
After the Revolution of 1912, the Nanjing Provisional Government transformed the Great Qing Bank—state bank of the Qing Dynasty into Bank of China. As the Nanjing Provisional Government moved the headquarter from Beijing to Shanghai in 1928, the old building was smashed and a new one was built. The building is in a decorative style: the exterior walls are decorated by blue stones; vertical lines and geometrical patterns are emphasized; the two parts of the top are in the shape of stairs; the block is covered with blue pyramidal multi-layered roof, with corbel brackets decorate the part under the roof. Reticulated flower windows are installed on the two sides of the front wall. It is the only high-rise on the Bund that has traditional Chinese decorations, and a large building designed by Chinese architect jointly with foreign architects.

✻ 3-North Building of Peace Hotel
Built in 1929
No. 20 Zhongshan Rd. (E1)
[Britain] designed by Gonghe foreign firm
The Peace Hotel (formerly known as the Sassoon House), was one of the real estates of Sassoon foreign firm and run by British Jews Victor Sassoon. One part of the architecture is in the shape of "A". With a steel framework, the 12-storied eastern block faces the Bund, and the western part is 9 storeys high. The building was built partly as offices of Sassoon foreign firm, and partly

as a hotel—the Huamao Hotel. The 4th floor are offices while the 5th to 7th is the hotel with English, French, Italian, Japanese, German, Indian, Spanish, American and Chinese style guestrooms. On the 8th floor there are a big bar and a dancing hall, beside which there is a rest corridor. In the middle of it there is a Chinese restaurant. On the 9th floor there are a smaller restaurant and a night club. The 10th is originally the residence of Sassoon, with British wood interior decorations. The walls of the architecture are inlaid with granite, in a simple and decorative style. The block is topped with a 10-m-high dark green and red-ridged pyramidal copper roof. Presently there is not only the North building of Peace Hotel in the building, but also the post office and shops on the first floor. Various guestrooms still exist but with renovated decorations.

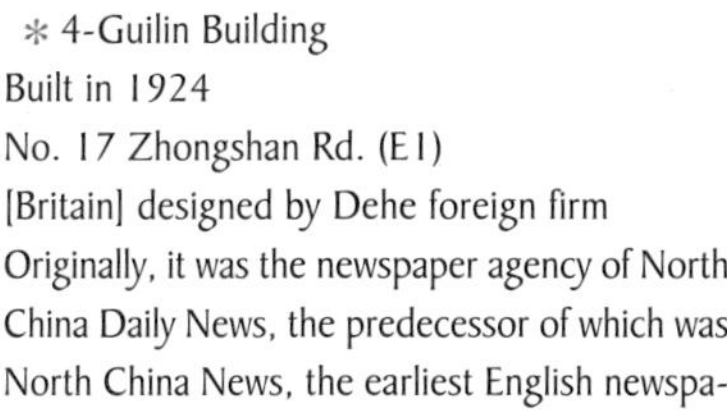

＊4-Guilin Building
Built in 1924
No. 17 Zhongshan Rd. (E1)
[Britain] designed by Dehe foreign firm
Originally, it was the newspaper agency of North China Daily News, the predecessor of which was North China News, the earliest English newspaper in Shanghai. The main building is 8-storied, but actually 11—counting the block, interlayer and the basement. It was among the first buildings in Shanghai that had more than 10 storeys. Facing the Bund, the front part is inlaid with granite. Roman Dorian columns and granite door decorated the entrance. On the top floor are there two Dorian columns. The facade was divided into three sections, in classic style, and was topped with Baroque block. It is of blending style.

＊5-Shang hai Customs House
built in 1927
No. 13 Zhongshan Rd. (E1)
[British] designed by Gonghe foreign firm
It is the site for Shanghai customs. In 1864, the Qing Dynasty government established here the customs in a wooden yamen-style house. In 1891, the old house was smashed and a 3-storied British Gothic house was erected in 1893, made up of bricks and wood. A British architect designed it, and Yang Sisheng, a craftsman in Pudong, arranged the construction. In 1925 the house was razed again and the present-day building was founded in 1927. The part which faces the Bund is 8-storied high, topped with 3-storied four-facet bell tower. The western part is 5-storied high. Both of them are of steel framework. The east walls, 1st and 2nd floors of west walls are constructed with granite, the 3rd and 4th of west walls are inlaid with brown tiles. Typical Greek Dorian columns stand at the entrance, a grand eave extended above the 7th floor. The upper part of the architecture is of decorative style. The position of the mast of 31°14'20.38" north latitude, 121°29'0.02" east longitude—the sign of Shanghai's geographical location.

FAVORITE SCENIC SPOTS

Architectures at the Bund

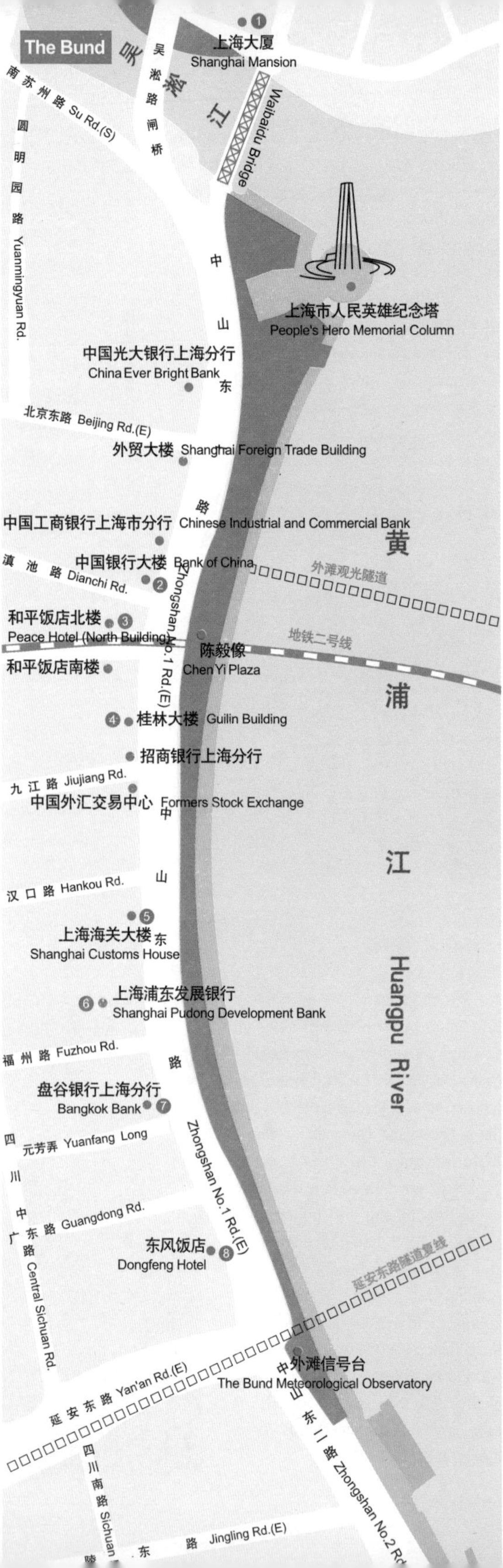

The Bund
1 上海大厦
Shanghai Mansion
吴淞江
吴淞路闸桥
Waibaidu Bridge
南苏州路 Su Rd.(S)
圆明园路 Yuanmingyuan Rd.
上海市人民英雄纪念塔
People's Hero Memorial Column
中国光大银行上海分行
China Ever Bright Bank
北京东路 Beijing Rd.(E)
外贸大楼 Shanghai Foreign Trade Building
中山东路
中国工商银行上海市分行 Chinese Industrial and Commercial Bank
中国银行大楼 Bank of China 2
滇池路 Dianchi Rd.
外滩观光隧道
和平饭店北楼 3
Peace Hotel (North Building)
地铁二号线
陈毅像
Chen Yi Plaza
和平饭店南楼
Zhongshan No.1 Rd.(E)
4 桂林大楼 Guilin Building
招商银行上海分行
九江路 Jiujiang Rd.
中国外汇交易中心 Formers Stock Exchange
汉口路 Hankou Rd.
5
上海海关大楼
Shanghai Customs House
6 上海浦东发展银行
Shanghai Pudong Development Bank
福州路 Fuzhou Rd.
盘谷银行上海分行
Bangkok Bank 7
元芳弄 Yuanfang Long
四川中路 Central Sichuan Rd.
广东路 Guangdong Rd.
Zhongshan No.1 Rd.(E)
东风饭店 8
Dongfeng Hotel
黄浦江
Huangpu River
延安东路隧道复线
外滩信号台
The Bund Meteorological Observatory
延安东路 Yan'an Rd.(E)
四川南路 Sichuan
中山东二路 Zhongshan No.2 Rd
东路 Jingling Rd.(E)

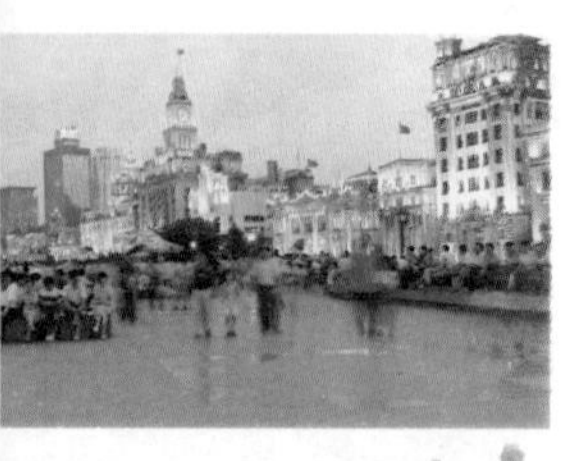

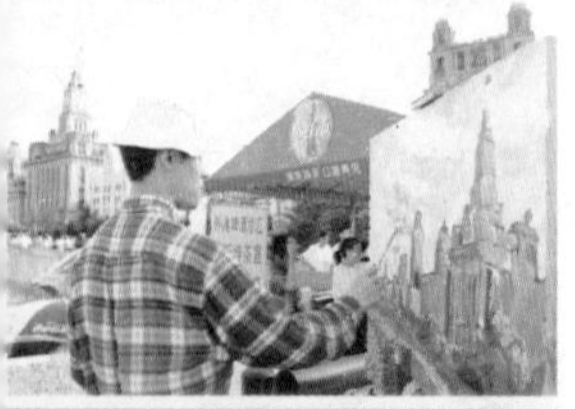

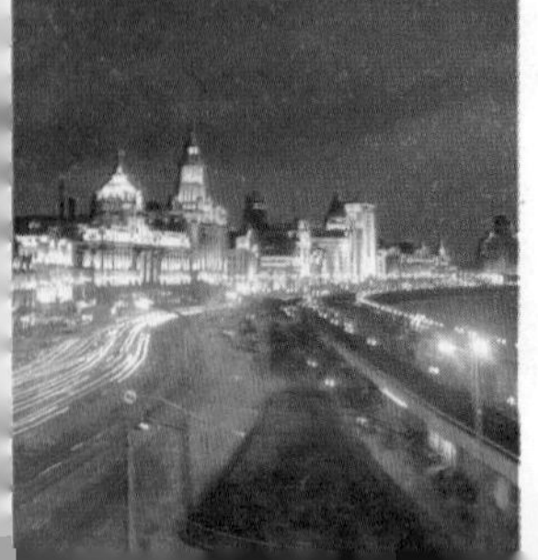

✻ 6-Shanghai Pudong Development Bank
Built in 1927
No. 10-12 Zhongshan Rd. (E1)
[British] designed by Gonghe foreign firm

Shanghai Pudong Development Bank (formerly the Hongkong & Shanghai Banking Corporation building). The former building was a 3-storied one, made up of bricks and wood. In 1921, it was smashed and the present-day building was erected, of reinforced concrete framework. The plane layout of the building is nearly a square. Its central part is two stories higher than the other part, topped with a steel dome. At the entrance, vertically beneath the dome, there is a round lobby, inside which is the business hall. The exteriors are in the style of rigid new classicism. The facade is horizontally divided into

5 sections, with double pseudo-roman-Corinthian columns running through the 2nd to 4th floor in the middle. Vertically, it is also divided by the roman columns. The top dome reminds us of the Pantheon in ancient Rome. On both sides of the front gate there used to be a pair of powerful and majestic bronze lions. The exterior walls are paved with granite. Arched glass ceiling and an ionic pillar carved out of Italian marble are in the business hall. Upon completion, the building gained fame as "the most exquisite building from Suez Cannel to Bering Strait". From the late 1950s to middle 1990s it was the office of Shanghai People's Government.

✻ 7-Bangkok Bank
Built in 1906
No. 7 Zhongshan Rd. (E1)
[British] designed by Tonghe foreign firm

It was formerly the office building of Foreign Dabei Cable Company, and was converted into the new office building of China Merchant Bank in the 1920s. It is now the Shanghai branch of

Bangkok Bank. On the 1st and 2nd floor is the Changjiang Hotel. The 4-storied house is of reinforced concrete framework. The facade is obviously divided into three sections, horizontally and vertically, with vaults on the top of the two sides. The whole architecture is in French Renaissance style, only at the entrance and the top are there Baroque decorations.

✻ 8-Dongfeng Hotel
Built in 1911
No. 2 Zhongshan Rd.
Designed by Mahai foreign firm

Originally it was the site of Shanghai Club, founded jointly by British merchants in Shanghai in 1861. In 1864 a 3-storied house of bricks and wood was built here. The present-day building was constructed after the old house was smashed, and was the earliest architecture with reinforced concrete framework in Shanghai. Including the block, the building has 5 storeys. Two pairs of Tuscan columns stand at the entrance, and pseudo-ionic columns run through the 2nd and 3rd floors in the middle. The whole architecture is in New Classicism style, but with Baroque window lintel decorations, wall decorations, and blocks. Marble stairway leads to the lobby on the 2nd floor. South of the 1st floor, there is the longest bar counter (about 110 inches) in the world.

CHEN YI PLAZA H16

陈毅广场

Zhongshan Rd. E1, end of Nanjing Rd.
中山东一路外滩和南京东路交汇处

At the end of Nanjing Road on the Bund is Chen Yi Plaza, on which stands the statue of Chen Yi, the first mayor of Shanghai in New China. The statue is cast with bronze, 5.6-m tall, standing on a 3.5-m pedestal of polished red granite.

The statue reproduces the image of Chen Yi while he is inspecting the work. His image of being an industrious public servant, and his meander of being affable and broad-minded are showed.

To the side of the statue is a fountain and the water columns are lit with the colored lights at the bottom of the fountain. At weekends there is an open-air concert on the plaza.

WAIBAIDU BRIDGE H16

外白渡桥

East Daming Rd. cross road of Huangpu Rd.
东大名路和黄浦路交汇处

Public buses 22, 37, 65, 20, 135, 145, 55, 61

Spanning over Suzhou Creek, Waibaidu Bridge is a well-known bridge. It was first built in 1855 of wood and rebuilt in 1907 in iron and steel. The bridge is 106.7-m-long, with a load of 20 tons, a traffic lane of 11.2-m-long and 3.5-m-wide sidewalks on both sides. It was once the most elegant and magnificent bridge in the city and, up to now, it is still considered as one of the symbols of Shanghai.

BUND SIGHTSEEING TUNNEL H16

外滩观光隧道

◆ The 646.7-m-long Sightseeing Tunnel at the Bund runs from the Bund at the end of Nanjing Road to the Oriental Pearl TV Tower in Pudong. It is the first of its kind for pedestrians in China. The tunnel adopts the internationally advanced SK system, taking 2.5-5 minutes. to cross the river. It is not only a new tourist attraction but also a means of transportation between the two banks. Its favorable location has made it a rainbow linking two banks.

- 20:00
- 22:30 (5.1~10.31), 22:00(11.1~4.30)
- oneway 30, return 40
- 021-58886000
- Pudong: No. 2789 Riverside Promenade
  Puxi: No. 300 Zhongshan Rd. E1
  浦东：滨江大道 2789 号
  浦西：中山东一路 300 号（外滩）
- Metro line No.2, Public buses 788 and 794
- 5 minutes

* It is the first sightseeing tunnel in China whose sights are created by hi-tech acoustic, light, and electrical facilities. The interior wall of the tunnel is decorated with changing colors of the yellow starfish, pink blossoms, different geometric designs, creatures of the globe by hi-tech means.

* The unmanned environmental, transparent carriages in the tunnel provide visitors with an open view. A 6-sound-band acoustic system accompanying the changing scenes, produces an effect on visitors of being present personally at the scene.

The automatic stairway in Puxi section is 11.7-m-high (as high as a 4-story building).

It is an easy access from the Bund to Lujiazui.

XINTIANDI L14

上海新天地

◆ The landmark of fashion in Shanghai, Xintiandi is an urban tourist attraction with strong flavor of Shanghai history and culture. It is the best place to feel and touch Shanghai yesterday, today and tomorrow, and is a leisure entertainment center integrating catering, shopping, performing functions of international standards.

021-63112288
Lane 181, Taichang Rd. 太仓路181弄
Metro line No.1 (Huangpi Rd. (S) Station) pulbic buses 42, 926, 911

* Located at the heart of the city, the Xintiandi Square is surrounded by Taicang Rd., Huangpi Rd. (S), Madang Rd. and Zizhong Rd. It neighbors commercial areas in Huanhai Rd. (M).

furnitures. Bar, Cafe shops, teahouses and Chinese restaurants coexist in a harmonious way. The modern paintings on the wall and the gramophone reveal the master's cultural taste.

* There are also a gallery established by a distinguished painter from Central Academy of Fine Arts, the Post Office Museum which has witnessed Chinese postal history, and the showroom of Shikumen residence which reproduces the life of a Shanghai family in the 1920s.

* When you walk into the Shikumen lanes, you will see the black brick sidewalks, red alternating with black brick walls, heavy lacquered doors, and door lintels with Baroque whorl flower, all of which remind you of the bygone days. However, when you step into the house, you see a completely different picture: the original partitions have been smashed to make a spacious room, with central air conditioner, European-style fireplace, sofa, and oriental traditional

* The "interior house" exhibition hall is a good place for us to reminisce about the old Shanghai and to trace history. It is converted from an old Shikumen residence built in the 1920s. With the storyline of a Shikumen family, it displays the unique Shikumen architectural culture in Shanghai, as well as reproduces the living space and lifestyle of Shanghai people then.

* In the south of Xintiandi there are mainly modern architectures, supplemented by Shikumen old architectures. A 65,000-sq.m. center is built, integrating shopping, entertainment, and leisure facilities. This modern looking architecture with glass walls is home to characteristic shops, including global restaurants, and the youth's favorite clothing exclusive shops, fashionable ornament shops, gourmet square, cinema, plus the largest one-stop gymnasium in Shanghai.

* Located south of Xintiandi is the 88 Xintiandi, an apartment with hotel services that embraces the Taipingqiao central green belt, and has a view of the largest lake in downtown area. The quietness is enjoyable. The considerate services make you feel free at home.

* Colorful man-made lake: This largest artificial lake in the heart of Shanghai joins the Shanghai Shikumen architectures on the west lake shore, forming a new landscape in the central city.

* Park: In Taipingqiao Park, big arbors are planted and low-slope landscape is built to provide a place for relaxation.

YUYUAN GARDEN K16

豫园

A famous classic garden in south China, it was once famed as the "top beauty in southeast China". First built during the Ming Dynasty, 400 years ago by a Sichuan Minister of Finance named Pan Yunduan, it has been several times renovated by the government since the Liberation and is now one of the key relic sites in the country under state protection. It was open to the public in 1961. The garden is divided into the scenic sections of "Mountains and Forests in the City", "Magnificent Woods and Beautiful Valleys", "Historical Relics of Heralding Spring", "Water and Rockery Scenery", "Tops in the World" and the Inner Garden.

- 9:00
- 17:00
- 30 yuan
- 021-63260830
- No. 132 Anren Rd. 安仁街132号
- Public buses 64, 24, 11 and 926
- about 60 minutes

In the west, the section of "Mountains and Forests in the City" consists of the Three Corn-Ear Hall, Rain Screening Tower, Giant Rockery and Emerald Green Hall. The predecessor of Three Corn-ears Hall was Happy Longevity Hall, meaning "happiness and longevity". On its roof

there are sculptures of Zhang Fei, Guan Yu, heroes in Romance of the Three Kingdoms. Dragons are decorated on the two sides, symbolizing authority and auspice. From the Rain Screening Tower one can see the Giant Rockery, beautiful lotus and the pond with gold fish swimming in it. On rainy days, visitors can see the big rockery shroud in mist, the tower is thus called the Rain Screening Tower. The Giant Rockery is the quintessence in the garden. It is a cultural relic of the Ming Dynasty designed by the famous horticulturist Zhang Nanyang.

✻ The section of "Magnificent Woods and Beautiful Valleys" consists of the Happy Fish Pavilion, the Double Corridor, Untied Boat and Chamber of Ten Thousand Blossoms. The Happy Fish Pavilion is of a typical gardening technique of Chinese classical gardens, an ingeniously designed relationship between space and the natural scenery, striking people as big in small. The door and window frames in the Ten Thousand Blossom Chamber are carved with the blossoms of the four seasons: the plum, the orchid, the bamboo and the chrysanthemum.

✻ The Spring Hall was once the headquarters of the Shanghai Small Sword Society in 1853. Kept in the hall are some of the cultural relics of the society, such as weapons, coins and announcements.

✻ The section of Water and Rockery Scenery consists of ponds and rockeries.

✻ The section of Tops in the World: There are the Exquisite Jade Stone, the Rockery and Water Corridor, Hall of Jade Magnificence, and the Dragon Circling Bridge. The Exquisite Jade Stone is one of the three famous big rockeries in China, noted for its wrinkled surface, slender shape, dripping holes and translucence. It is said that it was left by the "imperial rock and flower convoy" of the emperor Huizhong in Song Dynasty.

✻ The Inner Garden, with an area of only 0.14 hectares, is a garden within a garden, small in size but complete with all the pavilions, terraces, chambers, halls, rockeries and ponds. The Quiet Viewing Hall is the main hall in the garden, and echoes Huanyun Chamber. On its roof there is a sculpture of Yue Fei, a famous general in the Song Dynasty. There are brick carvings and clay sculpture everywhere in the garden.

MID-LAKE PAVILION AND THE NINE-CORNERED ZIGZAG BRIDGE K16

湖心亭九曲桥

◆ Mid-lake pavilion

As a symbolic architecture of Shanghai's opening as a treaty port, the mid-lake pavilion erects at the center of the lotus pond of Nine-cornered Bridge. It enjoys a history of more than 200 years. First founded in the 48 year of the reign of Emperor Qianlong in the Qing Dynasty (1784), it was one sight in Yuyuan Garden—a private garden of Pan Yunduan, the Sichuan Minister of Finance. It was once a place for clothing merchants' meeting, and was then converted into a teahouse in 1855, with names like "Yeshi Xuan" and "Wanzai Xuan", boasting the oldest teahouse preserved in Shanghai.

021-63736950

No. 257 Yuyuan Rd. 豫园景区内

In most gardens in South China the bridges are always zigzaged. In ancient China – "nine" – was considered the highest number, symbolizing a great number and magnificent scale. The zigzag bridges are designed to partition the water surface to enable visitors to enjoy the scene of the swimming fish in the pond, the lotus and the scenery in the distance on both sides. Traditional folk festivals are held here every year, such as the Lantern Festival, or the Yuanxiao, on the 15th day of the first lunar month. The place is crowded with thousands of visitors in an atmosphere of liveliness and festivity.

- 021-63554831
- In Yuyuan Commercial Bazaar
- Public buses 11, 42, 64, 66,126 and 926
- about 30 minutes

ANCIENT CITY PARK K16

古城公园

The Ancient City Park located at the intersection of Renmin Road and Henan Road (S), is part of the landscaped area around the old areas in Shanghai. Together with Yuyuan Garden, a complete and typical southern garden in China is formed here.

- 021-63366016
- No. 333 Renmin Rd. 人民路 333 号
- Public buses 11, 66, 71, 127
- about 20 minutes

SHANGHAI OLD STREET K16

上海老街

◆ The 825-m-long Old Street (formerly known as Fangbang Road (M)) runs from Renmin Road to Henan Road (S). From west to east, the architectures exhibit the changes of history and culture in Shanghai from the Ming and Qing Dynasties to the Republic of China. The commerce here is featured with traditional goods and Shanghai culture. It is a distinctive street in the Yuyuan commercial bazaar. In old Shanghai, it integrated tourism, sightseeing, shopping, entertainment and culture exhibition. You may find here the private banks, gold shops, jewelry stores, wine shops, tea houses, theatres, and other firms, usually called the center of all trades in Shanghai. Here, now, we can find some of the traditional trades like a coin store, old-fashioned tea houses, a shop selling mahogany decorative articles, a pawn shop, a wine shop, embroidery store and a private bank.

9:00

23:00

021-63281796

Fangbang Rd. (M) (Zhonghua Rd. to Henan Rd.) 方浜中路（中华路－河南南路）

Public buses 11, 42, 64, 66, 126 and 926

60 minutes

✻ The eastern section of the street has been renovated and restored to its ancient style. The aluminum screen doors have been replaced with checkered windows, wooden board doors and swing wooden doors. There are the old-fashioned drain pipes and upturned eaves on the roofs.

✻ In the western section the buildings are redesigned in the Ming and Qing Dynasties architectural style with black tiles and white-washed walls, red pillars and upturned eaves.

✻ Shops with a history of more than 100 years line up the street, like the Tong Hanchun, Old Tongsheng, Wu Liangcai, Wan Youquan, Qiu Tianbao, Old Shanghai Tea House, Deshun Restaurant, Dingniangzi Cotton Cloth Store, Rongshun Hall, Boyintang, etc. Shops with traditional features are also established, like Danfeng Tea House, Mingyitang, etc. Together with the "star street" in the north, it shows the lifestyle of all trades in old Shanghai.

YUYUAN COMMERCIAL BAZAAR K16
豫园商城

◆ The commercial bazaar, located in Yuyuan Garden tourism and commercial area consists of the famous classical garden in south China–Yuyuan Garden, the "kingdom of small articles of daily use", and the "kingdom of snacks", the latter two were flourished during the reign of the emperor of Tongzhi in Qing Dynasty. There you will find the Old City God Temple, the historical relic temple of Chenxiangge and the earliest mosque in Shanghai. It is thus a multitude of garden, market and temple. A large number of rebuilt Ming and Qing Dynasties-style buildings, together with the Nine-cornered Zigzag Bridge, Mid-

lake Pavilion and Lotus Pond form an attractive scene for tourists. When night falls and lights are on, the area is attracting visitors with its glistening beauty. It is praised as one of the "ten new landscapes in Shanghai in the 1990s". In the midst of competition in business Yuyuan Commercial Bazaar has become a hot spot for tourism, shopping and investment.

9:00

21:00

Fangbang Rd. (M) (Henan Rd. (M)-Remin Rd.-Anren Rd.)
方浜中路（河南南路－人民路－安仁街）

Public buses 11, 66, 71 and 127

HUANGPU RIVER CRUISE J16

黄浦江游览

The river cruise is an important traditional tourist item in Shanghai. The Huangpu River is the mother river of Shanghai. It symbolizes Shanghai and presents visitors with the cream of the city's scenic sights on its banks. Here you will have a glimpse of Shanghai's past and look into the bright future of the city. Starting from the Bund the yacht will bring you upstream to Nanpu Bridge, turn around downstream to Yangpu Bridge and all the way to Wusong Mouth, where the river meets the Yangtze, and then turns back.

The cruise company, with assets of over 1 billion yuan, owns different kinds of cruise ships, wharves of nearly 100-m-long waiting lounge of nearly 200 sq. m.; and enjoys the reputation of "Huangpu River cruise, window of Shanghai". The company offers boat trips to Wusong Mouth to see the Three Layer-Water, Yangpu Bridge, Nanpu Bridge, the cruise of the "Twin Dragons Playing with the Pearl", boat charter service and special cruises as required by tourists. With these it will embrace the coming of a "century tour of China".

9:00
22:00
45-100 yuan
021-63744461
No. 153, 219-239 Zhongshan Rd. (E2)
中山东二路 153 号，219-239 号
Public buses 20, 22, 42, 55, 65 and 71
45, 60, 180 minutes

* Twin Dragons Playing with the Pearl—Cruise "Twin Dragons Playing with the Pearl" will bring visitors to the two bridges of Yangpu and Nanpu, the Oriental Pearl TV Tower. The two bridges resemble two giant dragons, and the TV Tower symbolizes a pearl.

* Three-layer water—Wusong Mouth is where Huangpu River and the Yangtze meet, and where they flow into the sea. At rising tide you will see the three different colored water, the gray from the Huangpu, the yellow from the Yangtze and the green from the sea.

SHANGHAI HUANGPU RIVER CRUISER CO.

The double-dragon "Huangpu Cruiser" is a large dragon-shaped cruiser built in the Chinese national style. It is 55.6-m-long, 17-m-wide and with a speed of 8 knots/h. There are 4 deckers in the ship; on the first and second deckers are served all kinds of Chinese and Western delicacies and entertainment; the third decker is partitioned into smaller cabins of different sizes; the top decker is for tourists to enjoy the beautiful scenery of the Bund on the river under the sunlight.
Cruise route: Jinmao Tower-Oriental Pearl TV Tower-the Bund-Nanpu Bridge-Yangpu Bridge-Gaoqiao-Wusong Mouth
Add: No. 239 Zhongshan Rd. (E2)
Tel: (021) 63744461

SHANGHAI FERRY WATER TRAVELLING BUS CO.

Shanghai Ferry Water Travelling Bus Co. is also a cruiser company that offers cruises on the Huangpu River. The cruisers are complete with all facilities and offer tourists with all the comforts and attentive service in a cozy and tasteful environment. While admiring the beautiful scenery along the river, tourists may also enjoy the delight of all the amenities on the ship.
Cruise route: The wharf at Jinling Rd. (E).-Nanpu Bridge-Dongchang Road Riverside Avenue Wharf.
Add: No. 127 Zhongshan Rd. (E2)
Tel: (021) 63214062

ORIENT INTERNATIONAL CRUISER CO.

The "Orient International" luxurious cruisers of the Orient International Cruiser Co. can accommodate 350 passengers. They offer cozy, elegant, safe and reliable accommodation in deluxe rooms with outdoor balconies for sightseeing, standard suite, a lobby for sightseeing and many recreational facilities. Tourists may enjoy first-class service here.

Add: No. 515 Zhongshan Rd. E2
Tel: (021) 58782846

SHANGHAI QIANGSHENG WATER TRAVEL CO.

The "Qiangsheng Cruiser" of Shanghai Qiangsheng Water Travel Co. is a cruiser with beautiful shape and complete up-to-date indoor facilities. The observation deck is fitted with large glass panels. It can also meet the needs of meetings and other business activities.

Add: No. 511 Zhongshan Rd. (E2) (Inside Shanghai Port Passengers Terminal)
Tel: (021) 63264898

* Means of transportation for sightseeing on water mainly consist of cruise routes between Nanpu Bridge and Yangpu Bridge and along the Huangpu River, berthing at the wharves of the Bund, and Jinling Rd. (E). in Puxi, and at wharves of Lujiazui, Dongchang Rd, and Nanpu Bridge in Pudong. Cruise route:

1. Water Bus sightseeing route: Jinling Rd. (E)-Dongjiadu; In Pudong: Dongchang Rd.-Nanmatou, 2 yuan for cruise between two stops and 12 yuan for the whole cruise
2. Sightseeing on water: Nanpu Bridge-Yangpu Bridge 9:00-21:00 every day

Time-table for stops during the operation of Water Sightseeing Bus

Jinling Rd. (E) stop	Dongjiadu stop	Dongjiadu stop	Jinling Rd. (E) stop
09:00	09:20	09:40	09:58
10:00	10:20	10:40	10:58
13:00	13:20	13:40	13:58
14:00	14:20	14:40	14:58
15:00	15:20	15:40	15:58
Dongchang Rd.	Nanmatou stop	Dongchang Rd.	
09:10	09:30	09:50	
10:10	10:30	10:50	
13:10	13:30	13:50	
14:10	14:30	14:50	
15:10	15:30	15:50	

Add: No. 127 Zhongshan Rd. (E2), Shanghai Postcode: 200002
Tel: (021) 63214062 63237755 Fax: (021)63214062

YANGPU BRIDGE G20

杨浦大桥

◆ Yangpu Bridge is the second bridge built over the Huangpu River in 1993 with a total length of 7,654 m and a span of 602 m. It is 1,172-m-long and 30.35 -m-wide in and with 6 traffic lanes. It is a slanting cable drawn bridge with double towers and the main tower in the shape of a reversed "Y". The daily traffic capacity is 45,000 motorized vehicles. In July, 1993 Deng Xiaoping wrote the name.

- 8:00
- 16:00
- 021-58854701
- 2175 Pudong Boulevard (Sightseeing Office) 浦东大道 2175 号（观光办公室）
- Public buses 81, 85, 870, 522, 574, 571, 592, Bridge lines 3 and 4
- about 30 minutes

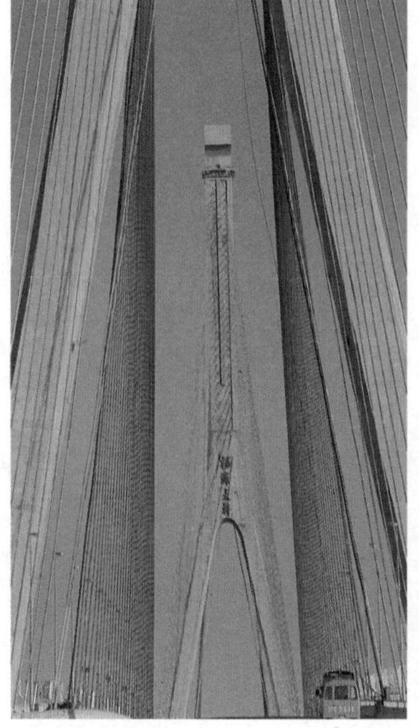

LUPU BRIDGE N15

卢浦大桥

◆ Lupu Bridge spans across the river like a rainbow, thus it is praised as "a rainbow bridge in the new century".

It is the 5th bridge over the Huangpu River, and is 8.7-km in length, 550-m in span, 41 m in height. It is a steel double-arched bridge, and is the longest steel arch bridge in the world, famed as the "world's No.1 steel arch bridge". It has become another symbolic architecture in Shanghai. During the construction period of 2 years plus 8 months, 10 world records have been created. The rainbow-like arch is welded by steel boxes. It is a breakthrough in bridge construction technology in history.

- 021-50565611
- No. 449 Yaohua Rd. 耀华路 499 号
- public buses 781, 786, Tunnel line No.2 and No.7
- about 30 minutes

NANPU BRIDGE M17

南浦大桥

With a total investment of RMB 820,000,000 Nanpu Bridge, completed in December 1991, was the first bridge over the Huangpu River in Shanghai. A cable-stayed bridge, with double towers and double cables, and overlapping ridges, it is 8,346 m in total length, 46-m in height, 423-m in span, 30.35 m in bridge width, and 846-m in bridge length. It is able to accommodate 50,000-t ship to pass through. The 150-m high tower is of reinforced concrete framework, in the shape of broken-line H. By the two sides of each tower, 22 pairs of cables, in a sector layout, connect the main bridge. The pedestal was built with groups of steel tubes which are 914-mm in diameter, over 50-m in length. 6 motorway lanes are set up to accommodate 45,000-50,000 motor vehicles. For visitors, there are 2-m wide sidewalks at each side of the main bridge, and also an elevator to reach the main bridge. On the bridge, is there "Nanpu Bridge"—the autograph by Deng Xiaoping.

The bridge approach is 7,500 m in total length—the Puxi section is 3,754 m in length, in a spire shape; and the Pudong section is 3,746 m in length, in a curve and round shape. The Pudong section links Pudong Rd. (S) and directly leads to Yanggao Rd. 6, 4, 2 lanes are set up in the bridge approach according to vehicle flow. The traffic speed is 40 km/h.

- 8:30
- 16:30
- 021-63763155
- No. 1410 Nanmatuo Rd. (Sightseeing Office) 南码头路 1410 号（观光办公室）
- Public buses 43, 65, 82, 83, 89, 109 and 868
- 30 minutes

Main memorials and former

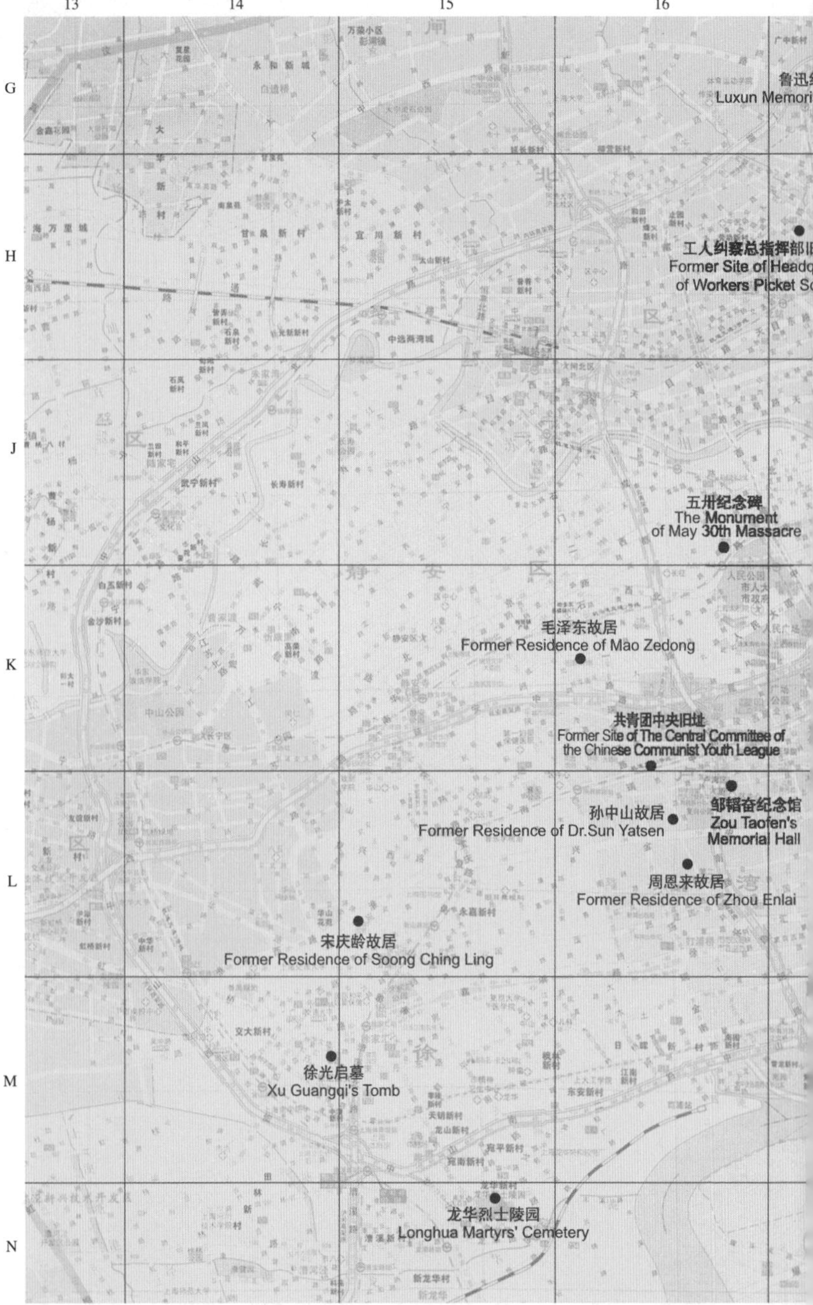

celebrities' residences in Shanghai

上海主要名人名宅、纪念馆

FORMER RESIDENCE OF DR SUN YATSEN L16

孙中山故居

◆ It is a two-storied villa with a lawn. On the first floor there are the dining room and sitting room. The second floor are the bedroom and study. Dr. Sun Yatsen and Madame Soong Ching-Ling lived here for 6 years from 1918 to 1924. Here, Dr. Sun conducted many of his revolutionary activities. He wrote many of his important works such as the "Program of Founding the Republic", "Sun Wen's Theories" and "Industrial Plans". In 1927, he called the meeting to sponsor the first coalition of the Nationalist Party and the Communist Party on the lawn. The building is listed as one of the key cultural relics under state protection.

- 9:00
- 16:30
- 8 yuan
- 021-64372954
- No. 7 Xiangshan Rd. 香山路 7 号
- Public buses 17, 24, 42, 926 and 911
- 30 minutes

SOONG CHING LING'S FORMER RESIDENCE AND MAUSOLEUM L15

宋庆龄故居、陵园

◆ It is a garden villa where Madame Soong Ching-Ling has lived and worked since 1948. She passed away on May 29, 1981 in Beijing. She was first buried in the International Cemetery together with the Song family. The cemetery was later extended and built into the mausoleum. In front of the tomb is the memorial square, on which a marble statue was erected in memory of her. There is also a memorial tablet carved out of granite.

Residence

- 13:00
- 16:00 (except weekends)
- 7 yuan
- 021-64376268
- No. 1843 Huaihai Rd. (M) 淮海中路1843号
- Public buses 126, 44, 48, 926 and 911
- 30 minutes

Mausoleum

- 8:30
- 17:00
- 5 yuan
- 021-62754034
- No. 21 Songyuan Rd. 宋园路 21 号
- Public buses 126, 44
- 30 minutes

FORMER RESIDENCE OF MAO ZEDONG K16

毛泽东故居

◆ Mao Zedong was a great leader of the Chinese people, a Marxist, a great proletarian revolutionary, strategist and theorist, the principal founder and leader of the Communist Party of China, of the People's Liberation Army and the People's Republic of China. The two-storied old-fashioned "shikumen" building was the residence of Mao Zedong in February 1924, when he came to Shanghai for the ninth visit. In June of the same year, his wife Yang Kaihui, her mother Xiang Zhenxi and sons Mao Anying and Mao Anqing came to live here until the end of the year. The house is now arranged as it was with all the articles of daily use in the former days.

- 8:30
- 16:00
- 5 yuan
- Lane 583, No. 5—9 Weihai Rd. 威海路583弄5～9号
- Public buses 49 and 23
- 30 minutes

FORMER RESIDENCE OF ZHOU ENLAI L16

周恩来故居

◆ Comrade Zhou Enlai was a great Marxist and Leninist, an outstanding leader of the Communist Party and the P. R. China and one of the founders of the P.L.A. The three-storied French-styled villa was the Shanghai office of the Chinese Communist Party delegation. In May 1946, in accordance with the "Double Tenth Agreement" with the Kuomintang, Zhou Enlai led the Communist delegation to Nanjing to conduct talks with the Kuomintang. In June, the delegation set up its Shanghai office here. The building was named the residence of General Zhou Enlai and also called Zhou's Mansion. Zhou Enlai had been to Shanghai four times. Here he held working meetings with reporters and met with patriotic democrats.

- 9:00
- 16:00
- 2 yuan
- 021-64730420
- No. 73 Sinan Rd. 思南路73号
- Tour line 10 Public buses 24, 17 and 96
- 30 minutes

LU XUN'S FORMER RESIDENCE, TOMB AND MEMORIAL HALL E17

鲁迅纪念馆、故居、墓地

◆ Lu Xun's former residence at No.9 Dalu Xincun, Shanyin Road, where Lu Xun lived from April 1933 to Oct. 19,1936 when he passed away. Here, he wrote many of his militant essays, translated the "Dead Souls" and compiled Ju Qiubai's posthumous work "Narrations on the Sea". The cultural relics on display introduce the process of Lu Xun's thought development, and emphasize on his social activities and cultural life during the 10 years he stayed in Shanghai.

Memorial Hall, Tomb

- 9:00
- 16:00
- 9 yuan (Memorial Hall)
- 021-65402288
- No. 146 Jiangwan Rd. (E) 东江湾路146号
- Public buses 18, 21 and 70, Tour line 10, light rail (Hongkou Football Stadium Station)
- 30 minutes

Residence

- 9:00
- 16:00
- 8 yuan (adult) 4 yuan (student)
- 021-56662608
- Lane 132, No. 9 Shanyin Rd. 山阴路132弄9号
- Public buses 18, 21 and 70
- about 30 minutes

ZOU TA OFEN MEMORIAL HALL L16

邹韬奋纪念馆

◆ It is a 3-storied alleyway residence, where Mr Zou Taofen lived from 1930 to 1936. On display are many of his manuscripts, works and inscriptions by state leaders.

- 9:00~13:00
- 11:00~16:00
- 1 yuan
- 021-63842811
- Lane 205, No. 54 Chongqing Rd. (S)
  重庆南路 205 弄 54 号
- Public buses 17, 24, 43, Bridge line 1, Tunnel line 8
- about 30 minutes

SANSHAN TRADE GUILD HALL L18

三山会馆

◆ It is a magnificent building of very high artistic standard. It was the site of the headquarters of the workers' picket corps of the Third Armed Uprising of Shanghai Workers. There is a folk collection exhibition hall in the building.

- 9:00
- 17:00
- 1.5 yuan
- 021-63135582
- No. 1551 Zhongshan Rd. (S)
  中山南路 1551 号
- Public buses 43, 89, 65,19, 929 Bridge line 2
- about 30 minutes

FORMER SITE OF THE CENTRAL COMMITTEE OF THE CHINESE COMMUNIST YOUTH LEAGUE K16

中国共产主义青年团中央机关旧址

◆ It was the place where the Shanghai Communist Group conducted its activities. On Aug. 22, 1920, the Communist Youth League of China was founded and set up its central organ here. It is now a key cultural relic under state protection.

- 021-64576327
- Lane 567, No. 6 Huaihai Rd. (M)
  淮海中路 567 弄 6 号
- Public buses 02, 42, 911 Tour line 10
- about 30minutes

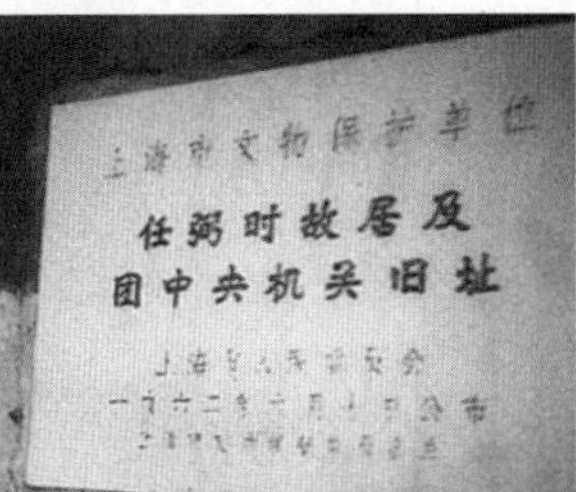

LONGHUA MARTYRS' CEMETERY N15
龙华烈士陵园

◆ Next to Longhua Temple, it was the place where the martyrs who gave up their lives. Buried there were over a thousand Communists and patriots imprisoned and executed here. Since the Liberation in 1949, the place has been preserved as a memorial site for the martyrs. In 1985, it was rebuilt into a martyrs' cemetery as approved by the Central Communist Party Committee and the State Council. It consists of the sections of Paying Respect, the Tomb Area, Hall for Ashes of Senior Cadres and Tablets. The site where the martyrs gave up their lives is now a key cultural relic site under state protection.

- 7:00
- 16:00
- 1 yuan (5 yuan for memorial hall)
- 021-65476327
- No. 2853 Longhua Rd. 龙华路 2853 号
- Public buses 73, 41, 44, 56, 104 and 864
- about 30 minutes

＊ In north of the cemetry there is a screen of granite wall engraved "Longhua Martyrs Monument", on the facade of which there is inscription by Mr. Jiang Zemin "They have devoted their lives for people". On its back side there is an epigraph. In the northern side there is "The memorial hall of Longhua Matrys", whose name was written by Mr. Chen Yun. Displayed in the hall are the heroic deeds of 235 matyrs who had fought in Shanghai, such as Peng Pai, Zhao Shiyan, Chen Yannian, Luo Yinong, Chen Boyun, Sun Bingwen, etc.

＊ Besides the cemetry, there are peach blossoms, red maple leaves, fragrant camphor trees, green grass and dozens of statues. The heroic spirit of martyrs was eulogized here. People are encouraged to make more contributions to the development of Shanghai and the prosperity of China.

THE MOMUMENT OF MAY 30TH MASSACRE J16

五卅纪念碑

◆ It is located in the green belt southwest of Nanjing Road (W) and Xizang Road (M). The tablet, ground and pedestal are all carved out of granite from Moutain Tai, implying that the matyrs' deaths outweigh Mountain Tai. The inscription was written by Chen Yun, and the epigraph by Lu Dingyi.

* May 30th Massacre: It happened on May 30th, 1925, in Nanjing Rd., in the public concession. On that day, 13 people died, and dozens of people were injured. It shocked the whole nation, brought forth May 30th movement. The Great Revolution then started. On December 7th 1977 it was listed as a revolutionary memorial site at the municipal level.

MEMORIAL HALL OF CHEN HUACHENG

陈化成纪念馆

◆ It is a base of youth education, where Chen Huacheng, the national hero who died for the country in the Opium War, was lively and artisticlly reproduced with video, acoustic, light, electrical facilities and manners of combining cultural relics and history, story and scenes.

- 6:00
- 17:00
- 2 yuan
- 021-56165854
- No. 1 Youyi Rd. (inside Linjiang Park)
  友谊路1号（临江公园内）
- public buses 53, 116, 508, 531, 541

MEMORIAL HALL OF SONGHU ANTI-JAPANESEWAR

淞沪抗战纪念馆

◆ Located inside Linjiang Park, Baoshan district, it is 53.6 m in height (12 floors)–A pagoda lies above the 4th floor. There is an observation deck on the 11th floor, from where you can see the mouth of the Yangtze River and Baoshan at distance.

- 2 yuan
- 021-66786322
- No.1 Youyi Rd., Baoshan district (Linjiang Park)
  宝山友谊路1号（临江公园内）
- public buses 53,207,508,531,541

HUANG DAOPO'S TOMB

黄道婆墓

◆ Huang Daopo, born in Wunijing, was an outstanding female who had renovated the textile technology in ancient China. Legend has it that she had drifted to Yazhou, and learnt the textile technology from the Li minority ethnic group. She renovated it, and went back home to impart the technology. She had made creative contributions to Chinese textile, and made Shanghai the center of textile industry in China. Her tomb was first built in Yuan Dynasty. In 1957, Shanghai people's government revamped it and erected a tablet. In 1962 it was restored and a white marble tablet was erected. In 1984 it was rebuilt again into a 1-hectare earth tomb with stone circle, blue brick ground, three walls and a white marble tablet with inscription of "Tomb of Huang Daopo", written by Wei Wenbo. In 1987 it was listed as a cultural relic to be protected at city level.

- 021-64830899
- No. 13 Dongwan Village, Huajin Town, Xuhui District 徐汇区华泾镇东湾村 13 号
- Public buses 50, 56 and 111
- 30 minutes

XU GUANGQI'S TOMB M14

徐光启墓

◆ Xu Guangqi, (1562–1633), was a scientist in the Ming Dynasty, the minister of Ministry of Rites in feudal China and Secretary of Wenyuan Pavilion. He engaged in studies of astronomy, calendar, irrigation works, survey, mathematics and agriculture. He introduced and absorbed western culture, and translated Guidebook to the Agriculture, History of Emperor Chongzhen and Geometric Original. He was buried at the confluence of Fahuajingbang and Zhaojiabang, where generations of his offspring lived, hence the name Xujiahui (meaning a gathering of Xu family). Rebuilt in 1957, the tomb was listed as a key national cultural relic under protection in January 13th, 1983.

- 6:00
- 18:00
- 021-64381780
- No. 17 Nandan Rd. 南丹路 17 号
- Public buses 93, 43 and 02
- 20 minutes

SITE OF THE PROVISIONARY GOVERNMENT OF THE REPUBLIC OF KOREA L17

大韩民国临时政府旧址

◆ Founded in 1925, it was the best-preserved "former site" where the provisional government had worked for the longest period. Here 3 Korea presidents and 3 speakers of congress had been received. The Provisional Government of Republic of Korea was called the holy place of Korea's national independence.

- 9:00
- 17:00 (except on Monday morning)
- 021-53824554
- lane 306, No. 4 Madang Rd. 马当路 306 弄 4 号
- Metro line No.1 (Huangpi Rd. (S) Station), public buses 17, 24,26, 42
- about 20 minutes

SHANGHAI OLD CITY WALL K17

上海旧城墙（大境阁）

◆ The wall was smashed in 1912 because it greatly undermined urban ecnomy and traffic. On its site are today's Zhonghua Road and Renmin Road.

It is a symbol to distinguish Shanghai old areas from the new areas.

- 021-63852443
- NO. 269 Dajing Rd, Xiao Beimen
  小北门大境阁 269 号
- Public buses 11 and 911
- about 30 minutes

* Dajing Pavilion: This is the only part preserved when the wall was smashed. It was formerly a watchtower. Later a temple in honor of Guan Gong, called God Guandi Temple, was built on it and still later a terrace was added to it. Now it has become a tourist attraction.

Main religion attractions

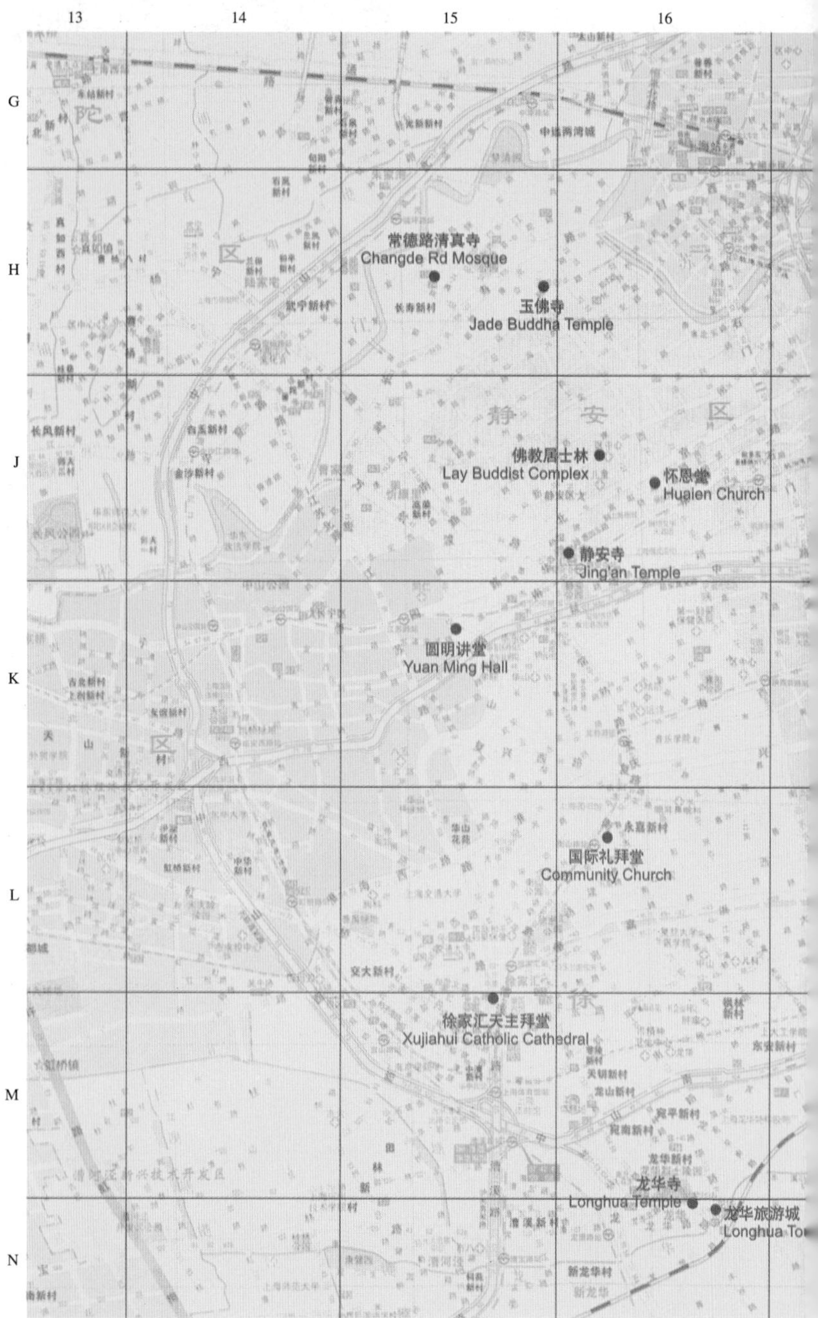

in central Shanghai

上海市区主要宗教胜地

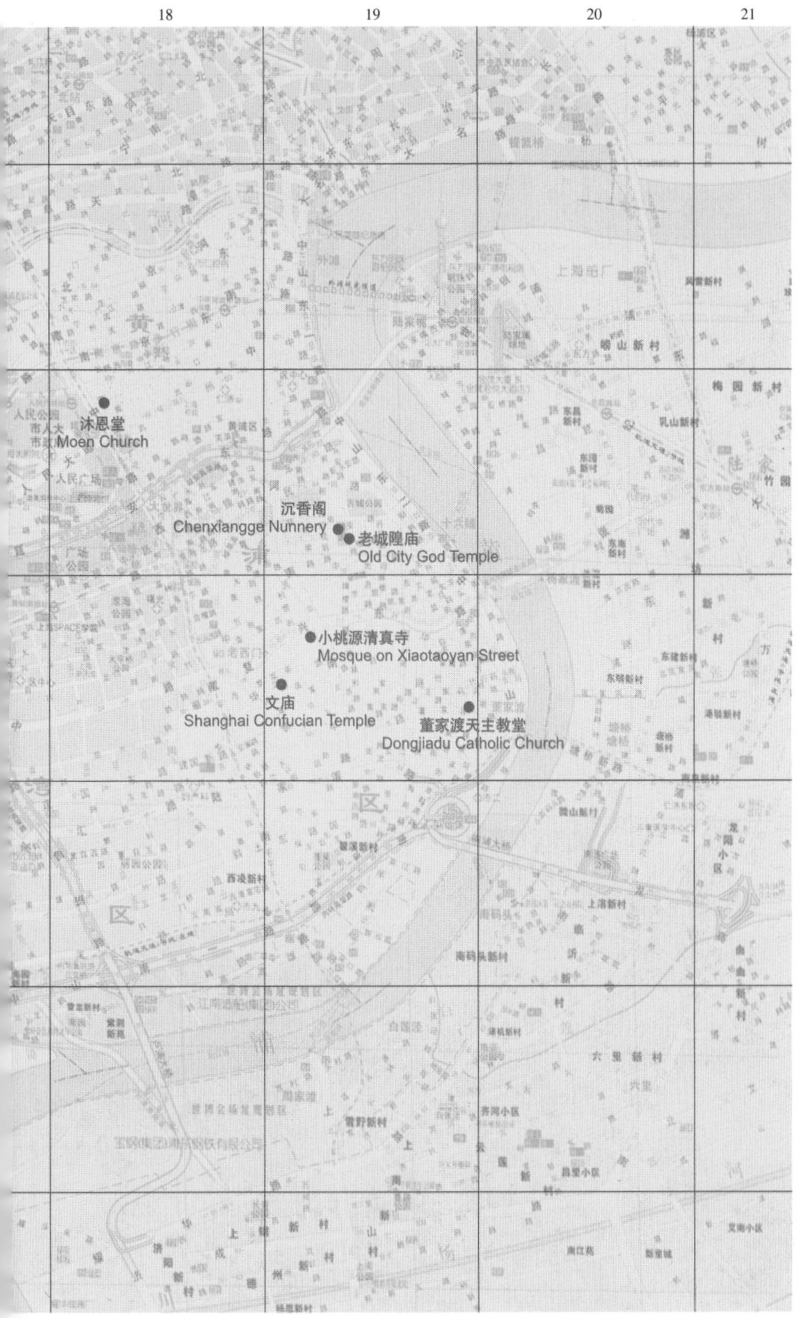

JADE BUDDHA TEMPLE H15

玉佛寺

◆ It is a famous temple known for the two jade Buddha statues enshrined in it. In 1882, the statues were brought to Shanghai by a high monk named Hui Gen from Burma, where he made pilgrimage and received jade statues of Sakyamuni. On his way back to China, he passed Shanghai and left a sitting and a reclining statue. In the 8th year of Quangxu's reign, in the Qing Dynasty a temple was built in Jiangwan to enshrine the statues, which ceased to funciton after the Revolution of 1911. A new magnificent temple of the Song Dynasty palace type was built in 1918 and completed in 1928 on the present site.

- 8:00 (pilgrimage periods 5:30)
- 17:00
- 10 yuan 5 yuan (1st and 15th date of lunar months)
- 021-62663668
- No. 170 Anyuan Rd. 安远路170号
- Public buses 19, 63, 76, 112 and 113
- about 60 minutes

* The 1-m long reclining jade statue is reclining on a mahogany couch in the reclining Buddha Hall. Resting on his right hand, the pleasant-looking Buddha lies on his side and looks up. It is the scene of the Buddha entering nirvana. It bears a composed expression, looking peaceful and free of worries.

* The 3.6-m-tall and 2.7-m-wide jade Buddha enshrined in the temple is the largest one of its kind in China. The 1.92-m-tall and 1.34-m-wide sitting statue is translucent and lustrous, solemn and magnificent. It is considered a rare piece of treasure, with ornaments—agates, emeralds, and precious stones adorned on its body.

* The temple keeps a complete set of 7,000 volumes of Buddhist scripture called "Da Zang Sutra" and other Buddhist relics.

* The vegetarian /restaurant in the temple is known for its dishes in culinary skill. Vegetarian food is considered one of the delicacies in Shanghai.

JING AN TMEPLE J16

静 安 寺

◆ It is a famous Buddhist monastery with a history of 1,700 years. Legend has it that it was first built during the Three Kingdoms Period and formerly named Huduchong-yuan temple. Its name was changed to Yongtaichan Temple in Tang Dynasty, and to Jing'an Temple until the first year of Dazhongxiangfu's reign during Northern Song Dynasty. "Eight scenic sections" remained in the temple until Yuan Dynasty; however, they disappeared in Qing Dynasty. After new China was founded, the people's government had funded twice for its restoration. It is now a comparatively complete temple under municipal protection.

7:30 (pilgrimage periods 5:00)~15:45

5 yuan (free in pilgrimage periods)

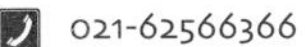

021-62566366

No. 1686 Nanjing Rd. (W)
南京西路 1686 号

Metro line No.1 & No.2 (Jing'an Temple station) Public buses 20 and 37

about 40 minutes

✻ The temple consists of the Mountain Gate, Heavenly King Hall, Three Sages Hall, Beneficence Hall and Abbot's Room. Above the Abbot's room a solemn-looking mandala was added, and in the left is the Chisong Rabbi. In the temple are such relics as a giant bell of the Ming Dynasty, stone Buddhist statues of Southern and Northern Dynasties, stone tablets and paintings by master painters Zhu Zhishan, Zhang Daqian and Wen Zhenming.

✻ The vegetarian restaurant in the temple is known for its dishes of vegetarian prawns, sea cucumber, fried plums, etc.

LONGHUA TEMPLE AND LONGHUA TOURISM CITY N16

龙华寺（龙华旅游城）

◆ Longhua is famous for "old temple, pagoda and peach blossoms". It has become a landmark scenic spot in Shanghai with rich local culture, revolutionary tradition culture and buddhism culture. Located in Longhua town, it is a famous 20,000 sq.m, and 1,000-year-old monastery in Shanghai, being the largest in scale and longest in history. It is said that the temple and Longhua Pagoda were built by King Sun Quan of the Wu Kingdom during the Period of the Three Kingdoms. It was rebuilt many times in the later dynasties. Many of the structures were built during the reign of Qing Emperors from Tongzhi to Guangxu. It has always been attracting large numbers of worshippers. The architectures in the temple are mostly built in the reign of Emperor Guangxu during Qing Dynasty.

* Longhua Pagoda, beside Longhua Temple, was also built during the Period of the Three Kingdoms. It was destroyed in war during the end of Tang Dynasty and rebuilt in the Northern Song Dynasty. Having been revamped in past dynasties, the present pagoda is a wood-and-brick, 7-storied, 40-m-tall structure. Graceful and attractive, it is the largest of the 16 pagodas in Shanghai, with a corridor and bells hanging on the eaves.

* Maitreya Hall, Heavenly King Temple, The Grand Hall, Three Sages Hall, Abbot's Room and Sutra Chamber line up the 194-meters-long central axis. On the two sides of Heavenly King temple there are drum towers 3-storied bell towers, with a bronze bell cast in the 20th year of Emperor Guangxu's reign during Qing Dynasty. "The tolling of Longhua bell in evening" was once one of the "eight sceneries in Shanghai".

Various precious cultural relics are collected in Sutra Chamber, including a gold seal conferred by the emperor, a Buddha statue, and 718 Buddhist Scripture granted by the Ming's Emperor Wanli—one of "three most precious treasures in the temple".

* In Longhua Temple, there are magnificent architectures, elegant flowers, precious musical instruments and epigraph by celebrities.

- 7:00
- 16:30
- 10 yuan
- 021-64576327
- No. 2853 Longhua Rd. 龙华路 2853 号
- Public buses 73, 87, 41, 44 and 104
- about 40 minutes

* Longhua Temple Fair, a folk festival with a history of more than 400 years, is held every year on the 3rd day of the March on lunar calendar.

* The bell tolling in Longhua temple "was better than the bell tolling in Hanshan temple", said Gui Mao in the Qing Dynasty. Now the bell tolling has been listed by Shanghai Tourism Department as a new tour of folk customs. It is advancing to the international tourism market, and thousands of tourists from Japan and Southeast Asia came here to listen to it.

OLD CITY GOD TEMPLE J19

老城隍庙

◆ First built in the reign of Emperor Yongle during the Ming Dynasty (1403), it is a major Taoist temple in Shanghai. In the temple there enshrines the City God Qin Yubo and General Huo Guang. It was very popular during the Qing Dynasty.

- 8:30 every day, 6:00 (on the lst and 15th day of the Lunar month)
- 16:40
- 5 yuan
- 021-63868649
- No. 1 Yicheng Rd. 邑城路 1 号
- Public buses 11, 42, 64, 66, 126 and 926
- about 30 minutes

CHENXIANGGE NUNNERY J19

沉 香 阁

◆ Formerly known as "Ciyunchan" temple, it is a typical Bhiksuni nunnery, a key cultural relic under state protection. There are the Heavenly King Hall, the Grand Hall, and the Chamber of Guanyin (Goddess of Mercy) line on the central axis, and on the two sides are the Jialan Hall and the memorial hall for high priest Yingci.

- 7:00
- 16:00
- 2 yuan
- 021-63203431
- No. 29 Chenxiangge Rd. 沉香阁路 29 号
- Public buses 11 and 66
- 30 minutes

WEN MIAO (CONFUCIUS TEMPLE) K19

文 庙

◆ The only Confucian temple in downtown Shanghai, it has been listed as a cultural relic under protection. Occupying an area of 17 *mu* (1 hectare=15 *mu*). It boasts Lingxing Gate, the Scripture Honored Chamber, a Setting Fish Free Pond and a lotus pond in the compound.

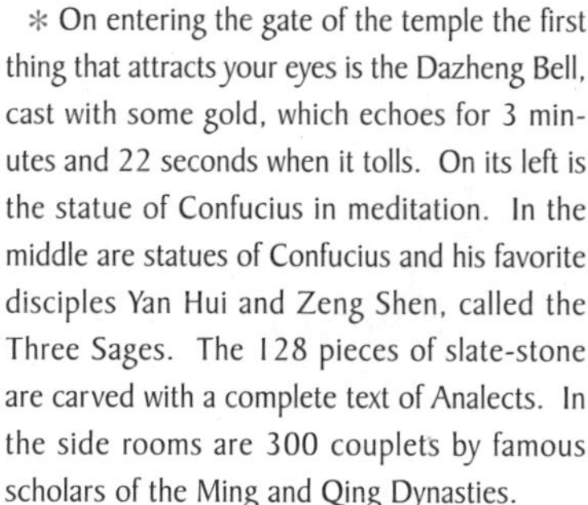

- 8:30
- 16:30
- 10 yuan (adult) 5 yuan (children)
- 021-63779282-3044
- No. 215 Wenmiao Rd. 文庙路 215 号
- Public buses 66
- about 30 minutes

* On entering the gate of the temple the first thing that attracts your eyes is the Dazheng Bell, cast with some gold, which echoes for 3 minutes and 22 seconds when it tolls. On its left is the statue of Confucius in meditation. In the middle are statues of Confucius and his favorite disciples Yan Hui and Zeng Shen, called the Three Sages. The 128 pieces of slate-stone are carved with a complete text of Analects. In the side rooms are 300 couplets by famous scholars of the Ming and Qing Dynasties.

* The buildings are typical expressions of the Confucius scholarly style. There is the Scripture Honored Chamber, partitioned by balustrades, with double upturned eaves, looking well-knit and solemn.

* In the east is the mysterious culture treasure: The Writing and Literature God's Pavilion, which

is scarcely known to Shanghai people. The ancient-looking temple, surrounding 100-years-old trees, mottled documents combine to add the temple's flavor of antiquity.

CONFUCIUS TEMPLE AND CONFUCIUS SQUARE

孔庙、孔子广场

◆ The over 780-years-old temple was first built in the 12th year of Emperor Jiading's reign in the Southern Song Dynasty. Through several times of renovation, rebuilding and extension later, it is praized as "No. 1 temple in the Wu Kingdom". In front of the temple there are the three memorial archways. The stone balustrades along the memorial archways are carved with 72 stone lions. The main hall in the temple is the magnificent Dacheng Hall, in which is placed a statue of Confucius and a complete inscribed volume of the "Analects". The carved inscriptions in the corridor of tablets are of archaeological value. The Exhibition of Cultural Relics of the Imperial Examinations vividly demonstrates to visitors the evolution, development and disappearance of the imperial examination system.

- Morning 8:00 Afternoon 13:00
- Morning 11:30 Afternoon 16:00
- 10 yuan
- 021-59530379
- No. 183 Nadajie St. 南大街 183 号
- Tour bus 6, public buses 517, 562, 822

CATHOLIC CATHEDRAL SHESHAN

佘山天主教堂

The catholic cathedral, or named the Cathedral of the Holy Virgin in China, is Romanesque church built in the 13th year of Emperor Tongzhi's reign during Qing dynasty (1857) on the top of Sheshan Hill in Songjiang District. It occupies an area of 6,700 sq.m. with a height of 20 m, looking magnificent. It is known as the "No.2 cathedral in East Asia". On every festival of the Holy Virgin in May, crowds of believers come in pilgrimage for masses.

- 8:00
- 16:30
- 021-57651651
- Sheshan Hill, Songjiang District 松江区佘山
- Tour bus No 1, Nanshe line
- about 30 minutes

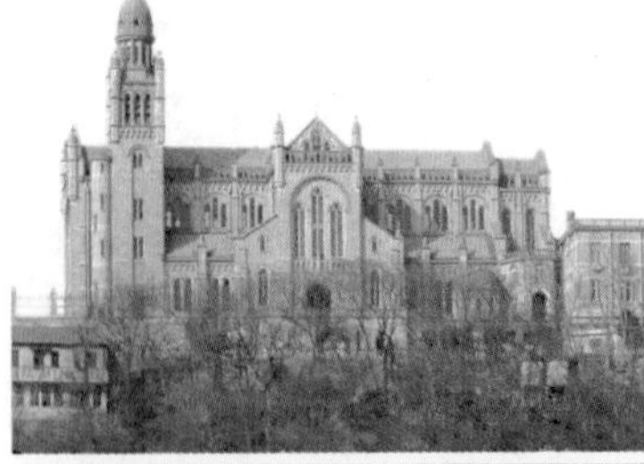

DONGJIADU CATHOLIC CHURCH K19

董家渡天主教堂

Located at Dongjiadu Road, Huangpu District, it is also named Catholic Church of Savorett. Built in 1853, it was then the first Catholic church in China. Well preserved up till today, it is a baroque architecture of the Renaissance style.

- 021-63787214
- No. 185 Dongjiadu Rd. 董家渡路185号
- Public buses 576, 868, 65 and 910
- about 20 minutes

XUJIAHUI CATHOLIC CATHEDRAL M15

徐家汇天主教堂

First built in 1896,the Xujiahui Catholic Cathedrale, an Episcopal church, is located in Caoxi Road (N). As one of Shanghai's culture relics under protection, it is a medieval Gothic architecture with 60-m-high bell tower. It is constructed with red bricks and framed with granite, looking magnificent and sedate with a divine atmosphere. On the front wall there is a large stained glass window. It used to be called "No.1 building in Shanghai". Before P. R. China was founded, it was the catholic center in southern China. It is now the religious center for Catholics in Shanghai, being able to hold over 2,000 worshippers.

- 6:00~7:00, 15:00~16:00
- 021-64690930
- No. 158 Puxi Rd. 浦西路158号
- Metro line No.1 (Xujiahui stop), public buses 15, 42 and 93
- about 30 minutes

HUAIEN CHURCH J16

怀恩堂

First founded in 1920, it was formerly located at the intersection of Liyang Rd. and Sichuan Road (N). It then moved to the present site. It is now a 2-storied red-brick house with a 1,700-seat auditorium and a bell tower in the southeast. In 1947, the Huai'en Spare Time Theology School was founded jointly with China Baptism, which was incorporated into China Lingxiu Theology Academy in 1955. On March 18th, 1994, Huaien Church is listed as an architecture under municipal protection.

- 9:00 on Saturdays and Sundays.
- 19:00 on Saturdays and Sundays.
- 021-62539394
- No. 375 Shanxi Rd. (N) 陕西北路375号
- Public buses 15, 21, 24, 41, 104, 37 and 20
- 20 minutes

MOEN CHURCH J18

沐恩堂

Located on the corner of Xizang Road, and Jiujiang Road, it faces the People's Park. The wood-and-brick Christian church has a grand bell tower. "Moen Church" means it is blessed by the God. It was first built in 1887 and formerly known as the Congregational Church. In 1990, it was renamed as Moen Church to commemorate the disciple Phillip Moen. In 1930 it was converted to a Gothic red-brick-structured church with music hall and an auditorium, capable of holding over 1,000 people. Social and cultural activities have been conducted here. Religious rites are held here on every Easter and Christmas. The East China Theological College is established in the hall.

7:00, 9:00, 14:00, 19:00 on Sundays (4 church services)

021-63225029

No. 316 Xizang Rd. (M) 西藏中路 316 号

Metro line No.1 and No.2 (People Square station), Public buses 18, 46, 49,145, 123 and 17

about 20 minutes

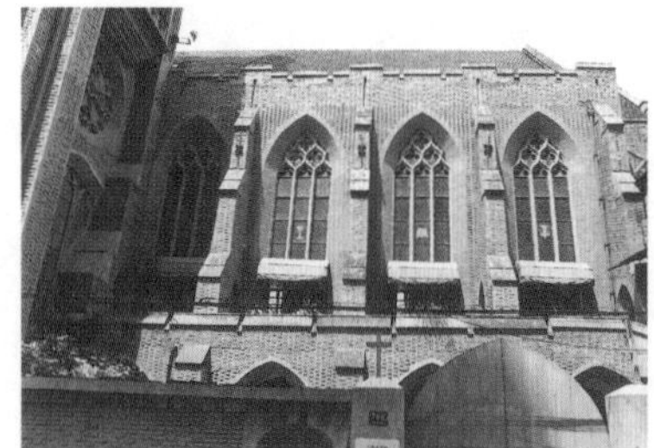

THE MEMORIAL HALL OF JUDAIC REFUGEES IN SHANGHAI

犹太难民在上海纪念馆

It is also called the Moses Hall. The residential areas of Jews during the Second World War have become the "second home" to the decedents of Judaic refugees.

 021-65120229

 No. 62 Changle Rd. 长阳路 62 号

 Public buses 22

COMMUNITY CHURCH L16

国际礼拜堂

◆ Located on Hengshan Road in Xuhui District, the church occupies an area of 7,300 sq.m. with a floor space of 1,372 sq.m. It is a modern Gothic wood-and-brick architecture with a cross shape roof. It can accommodate 1,400 people and is the largest Christian church in Shanghai. One of its features is the state Christian church without distinction of religious sects.

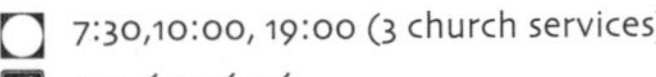

- 7:30,10:00, 19:00 (3 church services)
- 021-64376576
- No. 53 Hengshan Rd. 衡山路 53 号
- Metro line No.1 (Hengshan Rd. Station), public buses 15, 126 and 93
- about 20 minutes

MOSQUE ON XIAOTAOYUAN STREET K19

小桃园清真寺

◆ Originally named West Mosque, it is also called Muslim Mosque in West City. It is a four-block Islamic architecture of west Asia with dome roofs.

* It is a major Islamic mosque in Shanghai, and the site of Shanghai Islamic Association. It was founded in 1917 by a Islamic Mu Tongren, and then converted in 1925 into an Islamic featured religious architecture following the idea of his friend Jin Ziyun. The main buildings there are the square Prayer Hall, in the center of which there is a tetragonal Wangyue Pavilion, where the Islamic signal Wangyue pole is erected. After several revamps after Shanghai's liberation, it has been restored into its magnificence of the old days and become an important place for Islamic followers in Shanghai.

- 9:00
- 20:00 (5 church services)
- 021-63775442
- No. 52 Xiaotaoyuan St., Fuxing Rd. (E) 复兴东路小桃园街 52 号
- Public buses 24, 66 and 64
- about 20 minutes

SHANGHAI ZOO K11

上海动物园

◆ Found in the western suburb of Shanghai, the 70-hectare large-scale zoo for keeping and displaying animals was converted from a golf course in 1954. It was named as "Western Suburb Park", and changed to "Shanghai Zoo" on the new year's day in 1981. The zoo is landscaped with luxuriant trees and plants and dotted with lakes and streams.

- 7:00
- 17:00
- 30 yuan
- 021-62687775
- No. 2381 Hongqiao Rd. 虹桥路 2381 号
- Tour bus 4, Public buses 48, 57, 833, 911 925 and 806
- about 60 minutes

* There are 65,000 plants of 385 species. It is one of the areas in Shanghai boasting the best ecological environment.

* The zoo consists of the Gold Fish Corridor, Giraffe Hall, Elephant Hall, Lion and Tiger Hill, Panda Hill, Gorilla Hall and Monkey Hill. Recently new buildings have been added to it, such as the Hall for Amphibians and Reptiles, Area for Herbivorous Animals, Hall for Different Apes, Hall for Sea Animals, a Veterinarian Hospital, and a Hall for Scientific Education. The zoo keeps over 3,000 heads of 500 species of animals. Among these there are over 200 species that can breed, including some rare species such as the giraffe, the zebra, the red-spotted gazelle, the takin, south China tiger, black leaf monkey, ring-tail fox, orient white stork, and speckled-beak pelican. In the past 30 years Shanghai Zoo has succeeded in breeding many rare species of birds and animals, contributing much to the scientific study of wildlife.

SHANGHAI WILD ANIMAL PARK

上海野生动物园

Shanghai Wild Animal Park, the first of its kind in China, was jointly set up by Shanghai Municipal Government and the National Forestry Bureau. Located in Sanzhao town, Nanhui County and occupying an area of 162 hectares (2,800 mu), it is a state 4A-grade tourist attraction. There are over 10,000 heads of 200 species of rare and precious animals in the world, including giraffe, zebra, gazelle and white rhino imported from abroad; there are also our first-grade-protection animals like panda, golden-haired monkey and south China tiger, etc.

8:00
17:00
90 yuan
021-58036000
Sanzhao Town, Nanhui County
南汇县三灶镇
Tour bus No.2
about 60 minutes

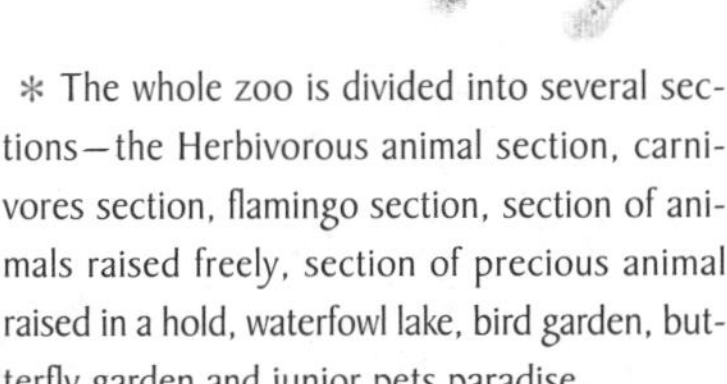

* The whole zoo is divided into several sections—the Herbivorous animal section, carnivores section, flamingo section, section of animals raised freely, section of precious animal raised in a hold, waterfowl lake, bird garden, butterfly garden and junior pets paradise.

* There are areas for visiting on foot or by car.

* In the area visiting by car, you may see the gentlemanly giraffe stretching out its long neck and expecting visitors. You may watch the largest mammal on earth—the elephant gently greeting you. There is the golden-haired takin, one of the three national treasures. On the way, you will see cheetah, the fastest runner in the world who can run as fast as 100 km/h; lion, king of beasts, revealing his majestic power while hunting for food; and "three clever ones", namely bear, monkey and fox, all coming forth to beg food from visitors. The powerful tiger inspects cars to go by.

* In the area visiting on foot you may see precious animals in the world, such as white lion, white tiger, white kangaroo, giant panda, and the Yangtze alligator. You may take pictures with the moose, camel, zebra and elephant. In the baby animal kingdom children may hug and feed the baby animals and feel the pleasure of seeing the breeding of the animal world.

* The animal show will entertain you with performances by man and animal actors. The sea lions' performances will bring you much delight and excitement.

SEA WORLD IN CHANGFENG PARK J13

大洋海底世界

◆ The Sea World is an aquarium attached to the Australian Ocean International Group with an investment of about USD25,000,000. Located in Changfeng Park in Shanghai, the aquarium was built on the bed of the Silvery Ax Lake, 13 m from the ground. There are over 10,000 fresh and sea water fishes of over 300 species and other aquatic creatures. The first theme aquarium in China, it was opened to the public in April 1999, and has so far hosted nearly 2,500,000 visitors. It is one of the favorite tourist attractions in Shanghai, and also a base for scientific education for youngsters. Besides, the aquarium has developed many services facilities, taking advantage of its own resources. The aquarium has set up a simulation airport, a historical site of the Peru Inca ancient temple, the Amazon valley and a fisherman's cottage on the seashore. The Sea World will open your eyes to the wonders of the sea and various precious sea creatures.

* Diving Club: It is the only professional diving training club in Shanghai.

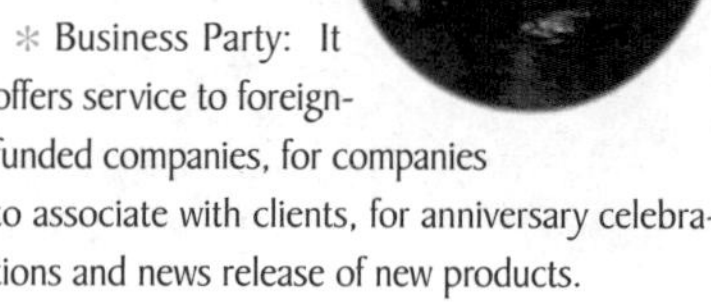

* Wedding on the seabed: It is a new form of wedding ceremony for young couples in Shanghai.

* Business Party: It offers service to foreign-funded companies, for companies to associate with clients, for anniversary celebrations and news release of new products.

* Overnight stay in the Aquarium: It provides overnight accommodation for children with the aquatic creatures so as to help them to gain more knowledge about the aquatic creatures and train them to explore the unknown world.

* Little Aquatic Division: It is an item for educating the children.

* There is a newly established recreational facility, the "mobile simulation submarine", opened to the public in August 2002. Besides the traditional feeding of fish by diving, there is the recently imported American seabed communication system, with which visitors may communicate with the divers. The construction of a performance hall for dolphins and sea lions is underway and will soon be opened to visitors.

- 9:00
- 18:00
- 80 yuan (ordinary) 100 yuan (VIP)
- 021-52818888
- No. 451 Daduhe Rd. 大渡河路451号
- Tour bus 6, Public buses 94, 837, 44, 67 and 754
- about 60 minutes

SHANGHAI BOTANAICAL GARDEN
上海植物园

◆ Built in 1974 and covering an area of 81 hectares, it is the largest city botanical garden in the country and grows over 3,000 kinds of plants. It consists of areas of Potted Landscape, Peony, Osmanthus, Rosebush, Maple, Pine and Cypress, Medicinal Herbs, Bamboo, and Orchids, boasting a speciality botanical garden integrating scientific research, science popularization education, sightseeing and production. The 4-hectare potted landscape area is the largest of its kind in the world, exhibiting over 2,000 fine works of Shanghai potted landscape.

8:00
17:00
50 yuan (joint ticket)
021-64513369
No. 1111 Longwu Rd. 龙吴路 1111 号
Public buses 56, 824 and 820
about 60 minutes

GREEN HOUSE IN SHANGHAI BOTANICAL GARDEN
上海植物园温室

◆ A newly-founded modern green house, it consists of Tropical Vegetation Hall and Desert Plant Hall.

8:00
16:00
40 yuan
021-64513369
No. 1111 Longwu Rd. 龙吴路 1111 号
Public buses 56, 824 and 820
about 60 minutes

* In the Tropical Vegetation Hall there is an all-season garden and a tropical rain forest, impressing people with true-to-life scenes.

* In the Desert Plant Hall there are different strange-shaped cactuses from all places in the world and precious fleshy plants with the background of a tropical wilderness, desert, camels and a setting sun, giving visitors a feeling of walking in the desert and experiencing the unfathomed mystery of the vegetation world.

* The Green House Exhibition, besides guiding visitors to the exhibits also provides a science laboratory to enable visitors, while admiring the beautiful scenery, to learn about the knowledge of plants.

GRAND VIEW GARDEN IN QINGPU COUNTY
青浦大观园

◆ Located 50-km away from downtown Shanghai and on the east shore of Dianshan Lake, it consists of east and west scenic sections. In the east, there are Shanghai Folk Custom Cultural Village, plum garden and osmanthus garden. In the west there is a large pseudo-archaic architecture complex which is reproduced, with Chinese traditional garden manners, from the Grand View Garden in the "The Dream of the Red Mansion".

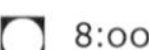 8:00

17:00 (March to October) 16:30 (November to Feburary)

50 yuan (busy season) 40 (slack season)

021-59262831

No. 701 Qingshang Highway, Qingpu
青浦青商公路 701 号

Tour bus No 4

60 minutes

＊Other scenic areas in the east: Plum Mound in Spring, Willowed Causeway at Spring Dawn, Golden and White Blossoms,etc. The Plum Mound in Spring in the garden is a place to admire plum blossoms.

＊Here visitors can have a taste of the Dream of Red Mansion banquet while listening to the Red Mansion tunes and admiring the Red Mansion buildings. Visitors may also dress up like characters in the "Dream of the Red Mansion".

DIANSHAN LAKE

淀山湖

Located in the west of Qingpu County and 50 km from downtown Shanghai, the lake covers an area of 62 sq.km., adjoining the provinces of Jiangsu and Zhejiang. A fresh, pure and clear lake, it belongs to the Lake Tai water system. Around the lake there are many little lakeside towns such as Jinze, Shangta and Xicen.

021-59716710
In west Qingpu District 青浦城区西侧
Tour bus 4

* The Sun and Moon Island on the lake is a tourist attraction for its favorable geographic location and beauty in natural scenery. On the island, birds are chirping, frogs are croaking, and the trees are lush green. In the lotus pond which covers an area of more than 4,000 sq.m., lotuses stretch their leaves to cover the whole water. On the 10,000-sq.m. water area you can appreciate natural landscape. Courtyard buildings are found amidst luxuriant trees and plants. The island offers tourists a special place of peace and tranquility.

* On the Sunny Island there is the 13,000-sq.m. International Club, consisting of an International Convention Center, a Celebrity Exhibition Hall, a business center, various recreational facilities, and several hundred guest rooms of different styles.

* There is the Water Sports Ground, the largest in the Far East, with up-to-date facilities of international standard. It is an A-grade yacht match ground and also for other competitions and training courses.

QUSHUI GARDEN (GARDEN OF MEANDERING STREAMS)

曲水园

Located in Qingpu County and first built in 1745, it was originally named as "Ling Garden", and then renamed as "Qushui Garden". It is one of the top five gardens in Shanghai, rivaling Yuyuan Garden, Guyi Garden, Qiuxia Garden and Drunken Bai pond. With a history of over 230 years, this unique garden has high artistic value of garden architecture in Jiangnan. It is centered on a pond with pavilions, terraces, chambers and bridges surrounding it, connected by long corridors and dotted with rockeries, pines and vines, all in a quiet and peaceful atmosphere. There are 24 scenes in all.

* In the North there are chains of rockeries.

* In the South there are the Ninghe Hall, Flower Goddess Temple.

* The lotus pond in the middle of the garden is surrounded by the Dawn Greeting Pavilion, Xiao Haoliang and Pleasant Rain Bridge.

6:00
17:00
2 yuan
021-59732996
No. 612 Garden Rd., Qingpu District
青浦城区公园路 612 号
Tour bus 4
about 30 minutes

ZHUJIAJIAO

古镇朱家角

◆ Known as "Venice in Shanghai", it is a well-preserved waterside ancient town. It was already a country fair as early as the period of The Three Kingdoms, over 1,700 years ago. During the reign of Emperor Wanli of the Ming Dynasty, with merchants flocking to the place and the population growing, it had become a prosperous town. There, we can still see the traces of the antique markets and streets of the Ming and Qing Dynasties. The antique buildings and simple life-style of the town's people will give visitors a feeling of peace and rest.

- 10 yuan (joint ticket 60 yuan)
- 021-59242771
- Zhujiajiao Town, Qingpu District
  青浦区朱家角镇
- Tour bus 4, Huzhu line
- about 120 minutes

* The town is crisscrossed by rivers. There are 3 bridges over the river among which the most famous one is the 5-opening stone bridge called "Setting Fish Free Bridge". Going back to history, the bridge was built in the 5th year during the reign of Emperor Longqing of the Ming Dynasty (1571) by a monk, forbidding people to fish but to set fish free here, thus it was named the "Bridge for Setting Fish Free". The bridge is 72-m-long, 7.4-m-high and 5-m-wide with 5 openings. The stone balustrades on the bridge are carved with dragon designs and on the top of each side are 4 stone lions. The bridge is of very fine workmanship, magnificent and exquisite.

* The little slate paths zigzaging through narrow streets, flanked by shops. They are like a scroll of Chinese ink and wash painting. A stone bridge over a flowing stream, flanked by dwellings of the Ming and Qing Dynasties, little boats slowly rowing under the bridge; the willows on the shores, plus the stone bridge—a scene of a peaceful life-style of antiquity and simplicity.

FENGJING

枫 泾

◆ Fengjing, an ancient town with a history of over 1,500 years, traverses Wu and Yue. A typical waterside town of South China, it has abundant rivers and streams in and around.

In Fengjing there are numerous bridges, temples, celebrities, alleyways and scores of river courses, over 50 ancient bridges and over 30 temples-all combine to form an unique ancient town landscape of "bridges in or beside temples".

With a profound cultural background, Fengjing is where many celebrities were born, such as the "three painters and one Go master", namely, the cartoonist Ding Cong, Chinese painting master Cheng Shifa, and Go player Gu Yongru. Besides, there are also the Jinshan farmers' paintings, which enjoy the fame as "precious folk arts in the world".

There are many famous and speciality products, among which the most famous ones are the four treasures: T-shaped hoof, Zhuangyuan cake, Tianxiang beancurd and yellow wine.

There will be more than 20 tourist attractions, over 10 of which have been completed, like Dingcong's Cartoon Hall, Sanbai Garden, Textile Mill, Folk Papercut, etc.

021-57355555

Fengjing town 枫泾镇

Shanghai lotus Station-Fengjing (non-station) (Shanghai Jinshan Bus Station) the bus starts every 15 minutes

about 120 minutes

QIUXIA GARDEN

秋 霞 圃

◆ Being a famous classic garden of South China and one of the top 5 gardens in Shanghai, Qiuxia Garden, with an area of 3.2 hectares and water area of 0.33 hectares, enjoys a history of nearly 500 years. It boasts 6,348 trees of 104 species. There are totally 48 scenic spots in the 4 scenic areas-Peach Blossom Pool area (the former Gong's Garden), Rosy Clouds Pavilion area (the former Shen's Garden), Clear Pond area (the former Jin's Garden) and Yiyi Temple area. The Rosy Clouds Pavilion has the best landscape in the garden.

The whole garden is of a compact layout, features fine workmanship. There are terraces, pavilions, chambers, ponds, balustrades, winding paths, slender bamboos,etc. The beautiful scenery gives the garden the name "urban mountains and forests". It can be traced back to the Ming Dynasty. The grand hall of the City God's Temple is also the exhibition center of Shanghai folk custom.

10 yuan (adult) 8 yuan (student)

021-59531949

No. 314 East Street, Jiading District
嘉定区东大街314号

public buses 517, 562, beijia line, 822, hutang line, tour bus 6A

ANCIENT TOWN OF QIBAO

古镇七宝

◆ In Qibao ancient town, the scenic sections of old streets are famed as "streets of Ming and Qing Dyansties in Metropolis" and "the living fossil of town's planning in ancient China".

There is a 360-m long south-north boulevard in the center of the ancient town. The North Square and the Bridgehead Square are the principal parts. An ancient bell tower stands at the entrance. There are tourists attractions such as archway, ancient theater in Qibao Temple, clock tower, tablets, Northern Street, Shadowgraph Showroom, textile showroom, Jieyuan Hall, Shaomu Pavilion, Zhenliu Pavillion, Anping Bridge, Eastern Pavilion, Zhangxun Pavilion, Kangle Bridge, Puxi Mill, Bifeng Terrace, Zhang Chongren Memorial Hall, wine shop, pawnshop, Catholic Hall, Puhuitang Bridge, Simian Hall, ancient ginkgo, Doumuge ancient theater and Qibao Temple.

The southern section of the boulevard is a street of catering service, offering visitors with all kinds of delicacies, such as the traditional Qibao square cake, mutton, Haitang cake, dried bean curd, etc. What needs to be mentioned is the Tangqiao snacks - soft and savory cake, sticky rice ball, fried bean curd, condensed bean curd jelly, baked sweet potato, etc. There is also another unrivaled bean product named black bean curd or black quilt, which is cooked together with game. The northern section of the boulevard is a cultural, tourist and shopping street, offering special local handicrafts, arts and crafts and commodities from other places, such as one treasure-cricket. Besides, folk handcrafts, like the handcraft knots, home-made cloth, broidery or seal carving show the profound local cultural tradition. Another feature in the ancient town is the puppet show. Beneath the archway in the old streets, handicraftsman gives performance in the stall. When there are enough visitors, the middle-aged actor begins to cry out, beating gongs. He wears special props to play two different roles in the Wresting, using his hands as the feet. With a history of about a thousand years, Qibao has many special local folk customs, like greeting gods, dancing with dragon lanterns, rowing dragon boats, cricket fighting, etc. The festivals vividly display the folk customs in Qibao.

Qibao District 七宝镇

Tour bus 1A, 1B, public buses 91, 92, 513, 803, Xinhua line, Nanjia line, Xinbei line

SQUARE PAGODA PARK IN SONGJIANG
松江方塔公园

◆ The 182-hectare Square Pagoda Park was built in 1978 and boasts a garden with cutural relic architectures.

There are 6 architectures in the garden under state, municipal and district protection respectively. The whole landscape centers on the square pagoda of Northern Song Dynasty, which is surrounded by scenic spots such as Wangxian bridge of Song Dynasty, Lanrui Hall of Ming Dynasty, Palace of Heavenly Princess of Qing Dynasty, Memorial Temple of Chen Huacheng, Hexagonal Pavilion, etc.

021-57838594

No. 235 Zhongshan Rd. (E), Songjiang District 松江区中山东路235号

Tour bus 1B, Hu-Song line, Hu-Song Freeway, Song-Mei line and Hu-Song special line

* The park is elegant, tranquil, clear and simple, blending modernity and style of Tang and Song Dynasties.

* The pagoda is 42.5-m high, 9-storied, wood-and-brick structure with the characteristics of the Tang Dynasty pagoda. It is a well-preserved Tang-style North Song Dynasty-pagoda, a typical wood-and-brick structure rarely found in China. On the wall of the third floor are preserved two Song-Dynasty-Buddha statue wall paintings, still quite distinct in lines and shapes.

* The screen wall was originally in front of a city god temple, built in the 3rd year of Emperor Hongwu's reign during the Ming Dynasty (1370). It is a bas-relief sculpture, 4.75-m high and 6.1-m wide. The bas-relief contents are preachings of Taoism. It is a cultural relic under municipal protection.

* Palace of Heavenly Princess was originally located on Henan Road, Shanghai, but was moved in 1980 to Square Pagoda Park in Songjiang. The building is of a palace type architecture.

CHANGXING ISLAND AND HENGSHA ISLAND
长兴岛、横沙岛

◆ The two beautiful Changxing and Hengsha Islands in Baoshan are now open to visitors. The islands face the river on three sides and the sea on one side. With fresh air and clean water and being away from the pollution of the city, they are ideal places of ecological reserve. On the wide expanse of the beaches are reeds and sugar canes. We can describe them as "with the river merging with the sea but not a trace of dust". Tides wash onshore shells and crustaceans and birds often come and perch in the marshes, bringing in so much life and vitality. In the home of oranges Changxing Island, visitors can boat in the reed marshes, have a taste or pick some oranges in the orchards and enjoy the delight of nature. They can also pick shells on the beaches or watch "birds flying over the setting sun in the clear sky and over the water of one color".

* In Shanghai, Hengsha Island is the best place for people to spend their holidays. Upon landing on the island, you will see bamboos and orange orchards—the natural scenery. Hengsha Hawaii Water Paradise is located at the east end, with clear water and soft beach, 10,000 sq.m. iron sand, and entertainment facilities like motorboating, surfing, water parachute, lover boat, etc., you will be able to appreciate the beautiful scenery on this fishing island, as well as to taste seafood or to have a picnic and BBQ. You will enjoy returning to the nature with the service

public buses 51, 116, 522, 728, 848, 849 and Tour bus 5 to Wusong wharf, and boat to Changxing and Hengsha island

facilities like nursing homes, holiday resorts, sea observation tower, sun greeting pavilion, etc.

* Home of oranges—Changxing Island

Changxing Island has always enjoyed the fame as "the home of tangerines" and "clear island". The favorite natural condition and rich natural resources have fuelled the development of Changxing tourism. The major sites are: Shanghai Orange Orchid, Mongolia Village horse race court, Chuizhu Garden, Shanghai Stunt City, Xianfeng Holiday Resorts, Shisha Wildlife Zoo, Green Island maze, Star Island Holiday Club, etc. Shanghai Orange Festival is held here every autumn.

GONGQING FOREST PARK

共青森林公园

Located in Yangpu District, northeast Shanghai, the 130-hectare park is facing the Huangpu River in the east. It is the only park in Shanghai featured by forest scenes.

Over 300,000 trees of over 90 species are planted here. There are totally 3 scenic sections in the garden: the forest section in the east, the riverside villages in the middle, with a water area of 90, 000 km, and the dense forests in the west.

- 6:00
- 17:00
- 12 yuan
- 021-65740586
- No. 2000 Jungong Rd., Yangpu District 杨浦区军工路2000号

DONGPING NATIONAL FOREST PARK

东平国家森林公园

Located in the mid-east part of the Chongming Island, the third largest island in China, it is the largest man-made forest on plains in East China, with an area of 358 hectares. It is also a well-known tourist area and one of the best tourist resorts in Shanghai.

- 8:00
- 17:00
- 30 yuan
- 021-59641841
- Dongping Farm in Chongming Island 崇明东平农场

DONGTAN RESERVATION AREA FOR MIGRANTS

东滩候鸟自然保护区

The reserve is in the east corner of Chongming Island, which has been formed by silt washed up from the Yangtse River. The total area is 450, 000 *mu*. It is still extending in size by the washed up silt at a rate of 150 m. (about 13 *mu*) a year.

* Dongtan was officially opened as a tourist area on Sep. 14, 2002. A giant rock was erected to mark the occasion, a landing bridge, built reaching out to the shoals, and a bamboo tower for watching the East Sea in the distance. Tourists may ride an ox cart on the beach and take a rest in lounges. Dongtan is no longer a mystery to visitors.

* The natural reserve for protecting migratory birds is the key tourist attraction in Chongming Island. As planned, a wetland park, an observation tower for watching the rising sun, a terrace for watching birds and a birds museum will be established. There will be participatory items by visitors like "visiting farmer families". Soon it will become a tourist resort for sightseeing, relaxation and amusement.

- Chongming Island 崇明东滩
- take boat at Wusong wharf (4 sails every day) or Baoyang wharf (10 sails) to Baozhen, then take Baoqian line

ORIENT LAND

东方绿舟

◆ Oriental Land, adjacent to Dianshan Lake, occupies an area of 5,600 *mu*. Covered by large tracts of water, lawns, woods and sculptures, it is an ideal place for young people and tourists to spend their holidays and do sightseeing. It is also the largest after-school camp for children.

* The camp consists of 9 sections: the Area of Bravery and Wisdom, the Thoroughfare of Knowledge, Education on National Defense, Challenge on Survival, Scientific Exploration, Water Sports, Sports Training, Practice in Life, and Aviation Activities.

8:30
17:00
50 yuan (adults)
45 yuan (students)
021-59233000
No. 6888 Huqingping Highway
沪青平公路6888号
Tour bus 4
about 45 minutes

* As a new tourist attraction for leisure and sightseeing in Shanghai suburbs, as well as the largest study and tour center in China, it boasts its beautiful scenery of vast water area, luxuriant greens, grand and magnificent architecture complex and multi-functional out-door activity facilities, which cater the needs of tourists of different ages and social status.

* Besides, the Oriental Land is the camp for youngsters' extra-curriculum activities, which centers on moral education, creativity and capability. It aims at improving the overall quality of youth, fostering their patriotism, collectivism, and their spirit of hard-working and cooperation. It is experimental and exemplary.

SHANGHAI FILM AND MOVIE AMUSEMENT PARK

上海影视乐园

◆ Located in Songjiang District, Shanghai Film and Movie Amusement Park reproduces truthfully and artistically the historical features and humanistic scenes of Shanghai. It enables people to learn about the evolution and development of the city.

* Here you will experience the life-style of old Shanghai. You will see the tram-cars that no longer exist in the city, the old-fashioned post office, tea house and pharmacy. It will enable you to retrospect on a part of the historical culture. At the same time, it is a place for shooting movies and TVs.

* 4 large and 3 small film studios, namely, "Old City of Shanghai", "Square of Film Stars", "Exposition Center", etc. will be built to provide scenes for filming. There will also be a man-made lake and a film studio on water, that will excite people with breath-taking scenes.

* In an old house named the "Museum of History of Chinese Costumes" there are exquisitely-made costumes and scenes of different times of Shanghai Film Studio, wax figures, army uniforms and "qipao" (ladies' dresses).

8:00
17:00
50 yuan
021-57601166
No. 4915 Beisong Rd., Chedun in Songjiang District 松江车墩镇北松公路4915号
Tour bus leaves Shanghai Stadium every day at 8:40 and comes back at 13:30. including transport and ticket or buses from Shanghai West Bus Station or The Subway at Jinjiang Amusement Park Station can also take you there

SHANGHAI FLOWERPORT

鲜花港

◆ Shanghai Flowerport is adjacent to Shanghai Airport in the south and links Shanghai New City in the north. It will be built into a supplementary area of Shanghai New City, a radiant area of Shanghai World Expo's horticulture and a pilot area of modern urban agriculture.

* The planned area is 100,000 sq.m., with 1 sq.m. as the core area. And the port will be divided into 4 sections.

* There are 3,200,000 tulips of 300 species planted here, displayed in an area of 28 hectares.

* East of the exhibition area, 3 windmills of traditional Chinese style are erected, showing a strong natural flavor. Various Chinese traditional wood bridges and houses are built in the garden.

60 yuan (open in March and April)
021-58295858 58291816
Donghai Farm in Nanhui District
南汇区东海农场
Line 2 in tourism hub
Metro line No.2 (Century Park Station)
Shidong line (Century Park—Donghai Farm) starts at 8:30, 9:20, 9:50 a.m every day

POND OF THE DRUNKEN POET LI BAI

醉白池

◆ Built in 1644 it is a garden of the Ming Dynasty and consists of the Inner Garden and the Outer Garden. The Inner Garden is the quintessence, with a square pond in the middle surrounded by pavilions, terraces, chambers and waterside pavilions, impressing visitors with its beautiful scenery. On the walls of the long corridor there are tablets carved with the calligraphy by famous calligraphers and painters.

7:00
17:00
12 yuan
021-57722415
No. 64 Renmin Rd. (S), Songjiang District
松江区人民南路64号
Tour bus 1, Husong line, Songmei line
about 20 minutes

GUYI GARDEN

古漪园

◆ Located in east Nanxiang Town, Jiading District, it was first built during Emperor Wanli's reign during the Ming Dynasty, and was formerly called "Yi Garden". The trees and rockeries were arranged by Zhu Sansong, the famous bamboo carver of the Ming Dynasty. The garden is remarkable for its historic sites and bamboos.

8:00 16:30
12 yuan
021-59124916
No. 218 Huyi Rd. Nanxiang town,
嘉定区南翔镇沪宜路218号
Jiading District Tour bus 6
40 minutes

✻ In the garden we will find halls, pavilions, stone boats, waterside pavilions, ancient trees, rare flowers, pebble paths and winding streams, all attracting visitors with their beauty and ingenious design. There are such scenic spots as the Hall of Pleasant Wilderness, Little Pine Mound, Little Cloudy Corner, Geese Playing Pond, Pavilion of Floating Clouds, Garden of Pine and Crane, Lake of Mandarine Ducks, Screen Wall of Nanxiang, Zigzag Bridge, Plum Pavilion, Mid-lake Pavilion, a scripture stele of the Tang Dynasty and a stone pagoda of the Song Dynasty.

JINJIANG AMUSEMENT PARK N14

锦江乐园

◆ A large modern amusement park in Shanghai, Jinjiang Amusement Park was opened in the 1980s. With an area of 110,000 sq.m., and boasting over 30 large and medium-sized amusement facilities, it is a wonderful multitude of entertain—ment, plastic arts and natural landscape. The tourists will enjoy themselves here.

* There are large amusement facilities such as a fem's wheel, a pulley car, laser shooting, flying disk boat, high platform speed changing sliding track, 45 wave dashing board, massage pond, etc.

* To meet the increasing needs of culture, entertainment and gymnastics of tourists from home and abroad, the park keeps introducing new facilities in recent years, such as the world leading facility—"Joy Land", "Drifting in Valleys", "Space Shuttle" and "Water Knight". The elevated sightseeing train—"Jinle Monorail Train" has been improved. In May 2002, the Chinese No.1 facility-the 108 m "Shanghai Grand Wheel" was finished. In May 2003, a large luxurious double carrousel has been finished.

- 8:30
- 17:00
- 60 yuan/30 yuan (joint ticket)
- 021-54200844
- No. 201 Hongmei Rd.
  虹梅路201号
- Metro line No.1 (Jinjiang Amusement Park Station), public buses 50, and 93, Xumin line
- about 60 minutes

City culture tour,featured streets of

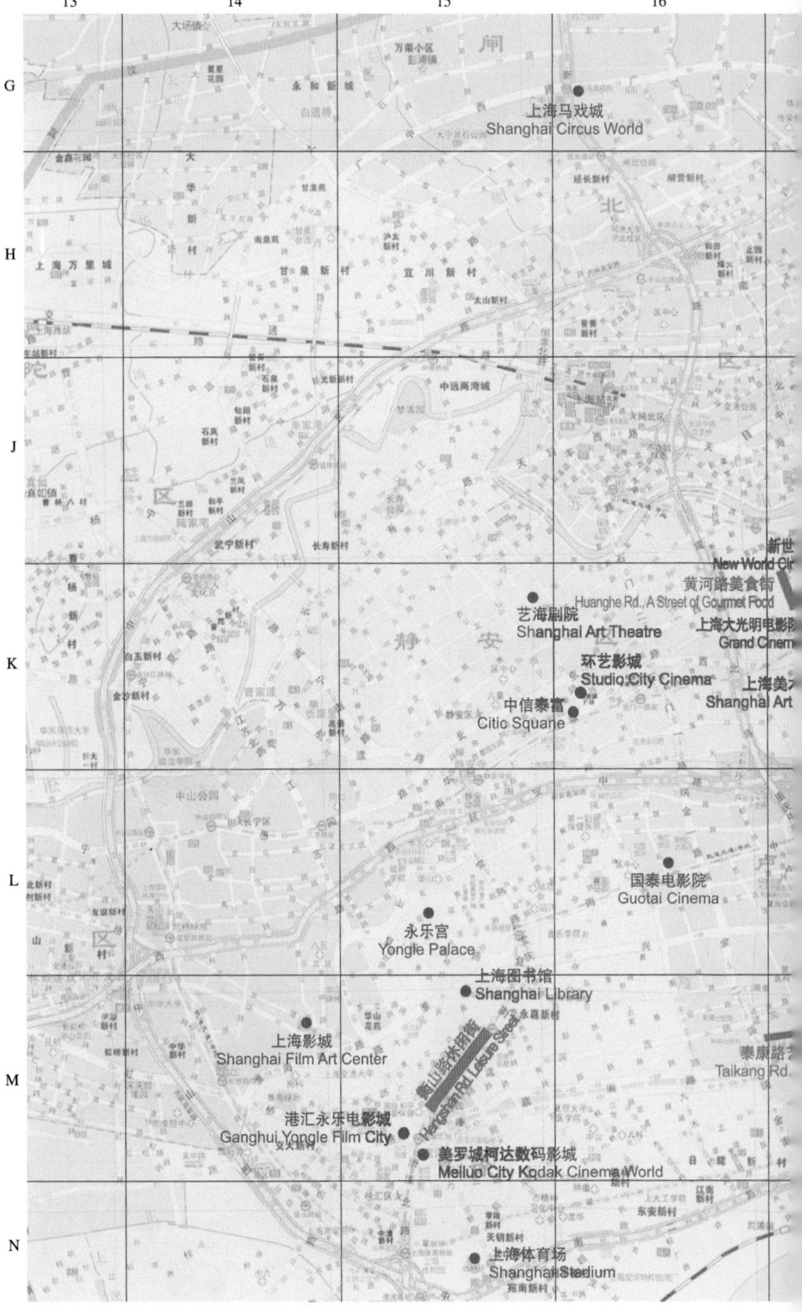

food &beverage and entertainment

都市文化线、餐饮娱乐特色街

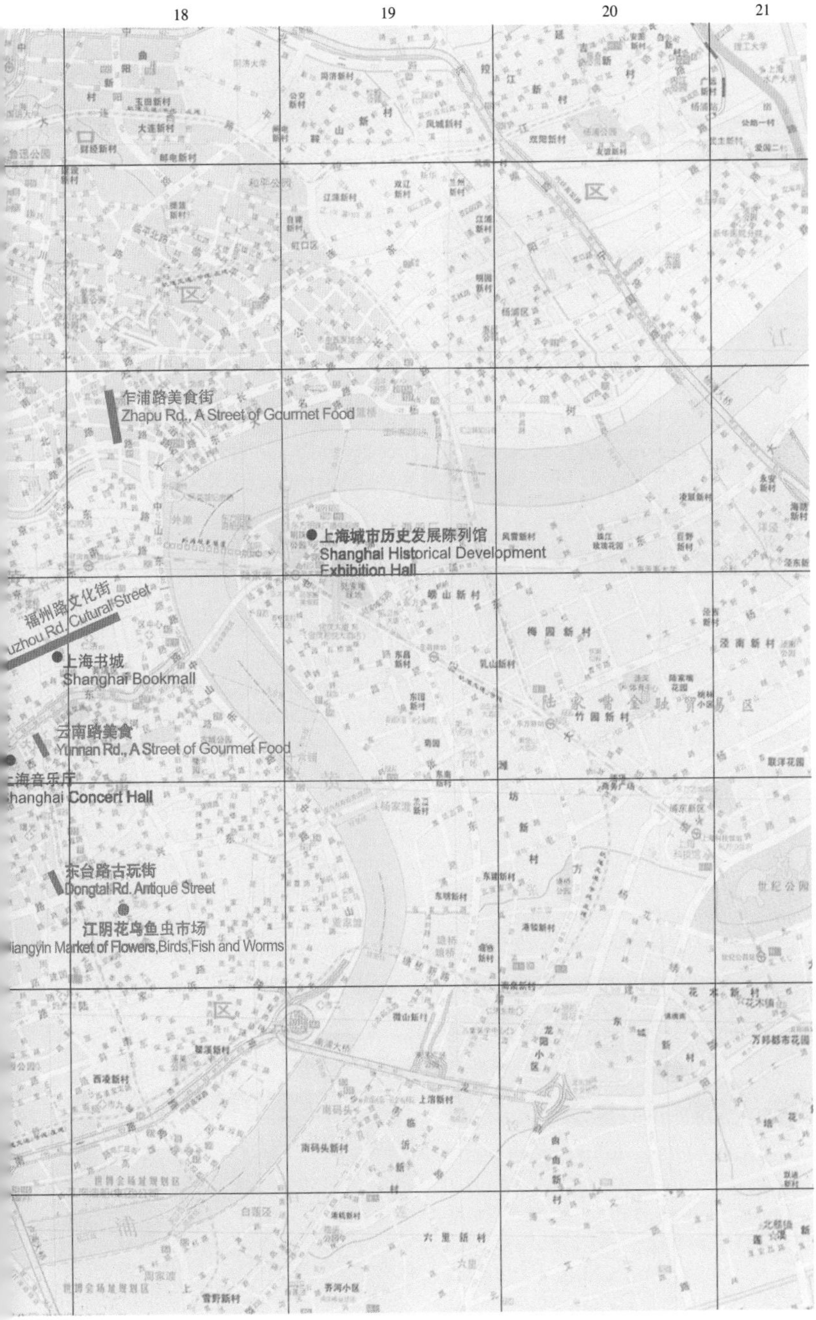

18
19
20
21
乍浦路美食街
Zhapu Rd., A Street of Gourmet Food
上海城市历史发展陈列馆
Shanghai Historical Development
Exhibition Hall
福州路文化街
uzhou Rd. Cutural Street
上海书城
Shanghai Bookmall
云南路美食
Yunnan Rd., A Street of Gourmet Food
上海音乐厅
hanghai Concert Hall
东台路古玩街
Dongtai Rd. Antique Street
江阴花鸟鱼虫市场
Jiangyin Market of Flowers,Birds,Fish and Worms
陆家嘴金融贸易区
世纪公园
万邦都市花园
六里新村
南码头新村

SHANGHAI HISTORICAL DEVELOPMENT EXHIBITION HALL
上海城市历史发展陈列馆

* See the introduction to interior Oriental Pearl TV Tower on P9

SHANGHAI BOOK CITY K17
上海书城

9:30

20:00
021-63914848
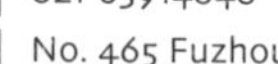
No. 465 Fuzhou Rd. 福州路 465 号
public buses 18, 49, 23, 46 and 66

◆ Magnificent and elegant and with a total operation area of over 10,000 sq. m., it is a extra-large retail bookstore in Shanghai, covering every major kind—life, Chinese and foreign literature, social science, culture and education, children's reading materials, science and technology and arts. Besides, the large volumes of books of Hongkong, Taiwan and foreign original editions give them access to the outside world. The service center on each floor also provides the readers with computer inquiry, managing mail and consign on readers' half. It also provides booking service.

SHANGHAI STADIUM N15
上海体育场

9:00 (a.m.) 13:00 (p.m.)

11:00 (a.m.) 16:00 (p.m.)

20 yuan (A ticket) 10 yuan (B ticket)

021-64266666
No. 666 Tianyaoqiao Rd. 天钥桥路666号

Metro line No.1 (Shanghai Stadium Station), Tour buses 1-10, Public buses 43, 72, 864, 401, 927 and 42

◆ The stadium was the principal sports ground for the 8th China National Games in 1997. Having derived from the world's advanced architectural achievements, the building has an elegant and novel style. The plane of the building is in a round shape and the elevation looks like a saddle. It expresses a strong modern flavor. It is the largest, most modernized stadium of international standard in China. It can accommodate 80,000 spectators. With most up-to-date facilities, it is not only unique in modeling but also complete in all functions for sports spectators and sightseers. Together with the 10,000-seat gymnasium and the natatorium next door, it forms a modern sports center in urban Shanghai.

The tourist attractions are: the torch, theme garden, underground VIP area, audience room, racetracks, lawn, rostrum, VIP box, 6.4 m platform, etc.

SHANGHAI LIBRARY M15

上海图书馆

◆ Occupying an area of over 80,000 sq.m. and with a collection of 13.2 million volumes of books, it is one of the symbolic buildings in Shanghai. It is now the largest library in China and listed as one of the world's largest 10 libraries. It ranks among the first in the country for its collection of modern Chinese and English magazines and newspapers, precious copies of the West, family genealogy, correspondences, rubbings and models for calligraphy.

8:30
20:30
10 yuan
021-64455555
No. 1555 Huaihai Rd. (M)
淮海中路 1555 号
Metro line No 1 (Hengshan Rd. Station), public buses 15, 93 and 126

* The library is the first to introduce the most up-to-date information management system of electronic library, coverage, indexing, circulation, continual publishing and public consultation controlled by the computer. It has also introduced the disk picture and script storage and different special data bases, and established an electronic reading room and a directory for city information.

* Books are arranged in an overseas "bookstore" style, changed from the past closed-up style, emphasizing on open borrowing. There are 23 reading rooms with more than 1 million books on open shelves. There are also 300,000-volume open shelves for 300,000 volumes of Chinese magazines and books for borrowing.

* There is a multi-media guiding system at the entrance. In the reading rooms and public areas there are different mini processors and public consulting terminals for readers to consult information.

The library has connected with the major networks in the country and abroad, providing readers with network services. Readers may obtain the necessary information at home. It is now the principal network and information center in Shanghai.

* Apart from these, there are a multi-function lecture hall and an exhibition hall, equipped with simultaneous interpretation and theatrical facilities open to the public.

SONGJIANG COLLEGE CITY
淞江大学城

◆ In the northwest of the new Songjiang City, close to Sheshan National Forest Park in the north and Songjiang Historical and Cultural City in the south, it occupies an area of more than 7,600 *mu*. A pilot place for open universities, it has a good cultural atmosphere and excellent environment for study and research.

* There are now on the campus Shanghai International Studies University, Shanghai Foreign Trade Istitute and Shanghai Lixin Accounting Institute. The East China Normal University, the University of the East Visual Arts Design and the East China University are making preparations to move into the compound. The college city's beautiful surroundings and up-to-date facilities are resources for all the schools to share. With scientific management it will be a really open unversity area for the independent universities to coexist harmoniously.

Song-Mei line, Hu-Song special line, Song-Xin line, Song-Qing line and Song-circle line

SHANGHAI GENERAL MOTORS
上海通用汽车

◆ Shanghai General Motors Co., Ltd. is up to now the largest joint venture of the Chinese automobile industry. It also has assembled the world's best technology of automobile products. Visitors may see, directly and clearly, the whole process of an empty car casing to a finished car driving down the assembly line. There are air sightseeing corridors built on the house frames circling the whole production area.

No. 1500 Shenjiang Rd., Jinqiao, Pudong
浦东金桥申江路 1500 号

* RECOMMENDED TOURS:

Tour A: Shanghai General Motors (lunch in factory) — Waigaoqiao Bonded Zone

Tour B: Shanghai General Motors (lunch in factory) — Shanghai Science and Technology Museum

Tour C: Shanghai General Motors (lunch in factory) — Lujiazui Finance and Trade Zone

Tour D: Shanghai General Motors (lunch in factory) — Sunqiao Modern Agricultural Development Area

SHANGHAI NAVY MUSEUM

海军上海博物馆

Located in the Wusong naval port, Shanghai Navy Museum occupies an area of 18,000 sq.m. Its name is the autograph of Mr. Jiang Zemin. Since its completion 10 years ago, it has received numerous young visitors. It is the national youth education base and a good place for war, national defence and patrotism education. It consists of Navy Junior School and 7 halls, like Marine Science Popularization Hall, Marine Arts Hall, Navy History Hall and Navy Weapons and Small Arms Shooting Hall, etc.

8:30

17:00

30 yuan

021-56163295

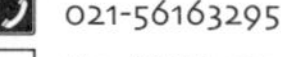

No. 68 Wusongtanghou Rd. 吴淞塘后路 68 号

Tour bus 5, public buses 51, 116, 711, 728

LIU HAISU ART MUSEUMLIU

刘海粟美术馆

A newly established state art museum, it is located on Hongqiao Road in western suburbs of Shanghai, with beautiful surroundings and convenient transportation. Though only 5,000 sq. m. in area, it is of modern shape, complete functions and advanced facilities. Inside there are 5 exhibition halls with first-class equipment, international convention center with visual, audio and simultaneous interpretation facilities of 5 languages. There are also galleries with constant temperature and humidity, public reading room, painting room, meeting room, gallery and Haishu Bookstore.

* The collection of the museum mainly consists of art works donated by Mr. Liu Haisu, including 364 calligraphy ad painting works he collected and 484 fine works of oil painting, Chinese painting, and calligraphy of his own. With some modern collection added, the number of collected items is now over 1,000.

9:00

16:00 (close on Monday)

15 yuan

021-62701018

No. 1660 Hongqiao Rd. 虹桥路 1660 号

public buses 57, 69, 925, 936, and 709

SHANGHAI CIRCUS WORLD G16

上海马戏城

◆ Reputed as "China's No.1 Circus World", it is a symbolic building in Shanghai and a symbol of Shanghai's status as an international cultural exchange center.

021-66527550

No. 2266 Gonghexin Rd. 共和新路2266号

Public buses 46, 95 and 114

* The main building of the circus city is in a unique shape of a golden sphere, which demostrates the city's characteristics. The entertainment city and supplementary houses are in a curve shape, echoing the main building, and convey a sense of modernity, harmony and magnificence.

* The Acrobatic Theater is the core area of Shanghai Circus World, with 1,638 seats and a performance height of 17 m. It is equipped with up-to-date light facility, multi-tone and multi-surround sound facility. In the performance area, there are rotating stage, elevating stage, frame-style stage and booms, 3 horse ways in the air--which combine to make it a completely-equippd, multi-function acrobatic performance place. Outstanding circus and acrobatic items from home and abroad are performed here.

* ERA - Intersection of Time

The Multimedia Theatrical Spectacular

As a multimillion-dollar stunning acrobatic extravaganza, the first of its kind in China, ERA is a multimedia odyssey whose inspiration is a direct result of the combination of traditional Chinese acrobatic arts and modern technology. Just like Shanghai, ERA evolves through a constant collision between the past and future.

ERA is a love story, yet it is also a contemplation across the millennia, a fascination with that other dimension man has yet to conquer: time. ERA's acrobats are on a quest to find that tenuous point of balance, the intersection between X, Y and Z.

Not only will the audience be amazed by the acrobats' control and precision, they will be enchanted by the world that is created through the use of multimedia, technology, lighting and sound effects, elaborate costumes, original live music and a lot more.

As such, ERA can remain universal, without language or cultural barriers. A thousand-year-old gesture is worth a thousand emotions, a thousand images, a thousand words.

Allow us to feed your imagination and bring your dreams back to the present.

SHANGHAI ART THEATRE K15

艺海剧院

◆ The theatre was built in 2001 on the corner of Jiangning Road and Kangding Road. "Yi Hai" in Chinese means the sea of art, implying "a sea gathering a hundred rivers", or in other words "a kingdom of a hundred artistic schools". Its establishment has emerged in the metropolis a modern and intelligent-type artistic theatre.

19:30

021-62720331

No. 466 Jiangning Rd. 江宁路466号

Public buses 23, 68, 112 and 36

SHANGHAI ORIENTAL ART CENTER

东方艺术中心

◆ Located in Pudong Administration and Culture Center, it is designed by a famous French architecture designer Paul Andrew, with a total floor area of 40,000 sq.m. It is a large cultural facility with the most complete and advanced equipment. Its shape resembles a huge "butterfly orchid" in full blossom. The exterior adopts sandwich glass walls, and the interior walls are decorated by special yellow, reddish brown, brown and gray ceramics ornaments.

* The center consists of Orient Music Hall with 1,966 seats, Orient Opera House with 1,020 seats, and Orient Performance Hall with 327 seats. There is the most advanced sound and light stage facilities, and a series of hi-tech facilities, such as the digital sound control, which is the most advanced in domestic theaters and wireless PDA conventional light control. They can meet the demands of symphony, ballet, melodrama, opera, and play performance.

NO. 425 Dingxiang Rd., Pudong 浦东丁香路425号

Metro line No.2 (Shanghai Science and Technology Museum Station), public buses 638, 640, 788, 794, 815, 983, 984, 987 and Dongzhou line

SHANGHAI FILM ART CENTER M14

上海影城

◆ It is a 5-star multi-functional cinema, offering entertainment, catering and meeting services.

- ☎ 021-62804088
- NO. 160 Xinhua Rd. 新华路 160 号
- Public buses 48, 76, 72, 113 and 138

* Distinctive features No.1 showroom: it is the main site for Shanghai International Film Festival. The 1,118-seat No.1 showroom is painted red with an international THX standard in acoustic design and has a 230-sq.m. screen, the first of its kind in China and comparable to world's first-rate cinemas. No.2 and No.3 showrooms are fitted the same as No.1 showroom, but with tastefully furnished environment. All the showrooms are provided with sofa seats and look elegant in taste.

STUDIO CITY CINEMA K16

环艺电影城

◆ It is a modernized, artistic and entertaining establishment of the latest fashion. The lobby is designed in a bold and novel style, emphasizing on space and light. It offers audience with such services as providing the latest news of films and letting audience to choose their own seats. It is equipped with the latest automatic projecting facilities and 8-tone digital acoustic device, producing excellent audio visual effect.

- ☎ 021-62182173, 021-62187109
-  10th Floor Meilong Square, NO. 1038 Nanjing Rd., (W)

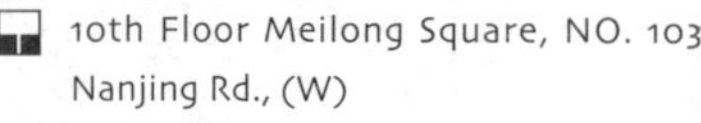

  南京西路 1038 号（梅龙镇广场 10 楼）
- Public buses 15, 20, 21, 37, 109 and 112

NEW WORLD CINEMA CITY K17

新世界电影城

◆ New World Cinema City is a 5-star international film city, built jointly by Shanghai Film Group Coperations (SFG) and Taiwan Huawei Film City, Co. Ltd. It is a modern multi-functional film city located in the highest floors in Shanghai. The first-class design, with 6 exquisite and luxurious film halls and no more than 50 seats in each hall makes you feel that it is your own box. The No.5 hall is super VIP hall, which is equipped with leather sofa. The star avenue on the 11th floor and large classic film posters create an artistic atmosphere.

The price is 50% off on Tuesday before 12:00 every day (excluding 12:00).

- ☎ 63594933, 63596810
- 12th floor New World City, No. 2~68 Nanjing Rd. (W)
  南京西路 2~68 号（新世界商城 11-12 楼）
- Metro line No.1 and No.2 (People Square Station)

KODAK CINEMA WORLD M15

柯达电影世界

◆ The first of its kind designed according to the standards of the American "Verification system of film projection quality", it is equipped with advanced projecting facilities and digital stereosonic effects. The seats are designed in a flexible way to enable the audience to adjust freely. The passages are broad, easy for the handicapped to move about. It also provides audiphones.

- ☎ 021-64268181
- 5th floor of Meiluo City, No. 1111 Zaojiabang Rd. 肇家浜路 1111 号（美罗城 5 楼）
- Metro line No.1 (Xujiahui Station), public buses 926, 920, 804, 820, 15, 43, 42, 72 and 44

＊ The encircling wall of the Cinema World is decorated with a 100-m-long posters of movies from China and foreign countries.

GRAND CINEMA K17

大光明电影院

◆ Enjoying the name of "No.1 Cinema in the Far East", it has an European-style architecture. It has been listed by the government as a fine modern building. Equipped with digital stereosonic facility, it produces extremely fine sound effect. Its film box has topped China ever since 11 years before.

＊ Plesant-looking architecture The exterior of the cinema in creamy color and attractive architectural style looks like a boat sailing in the sea. The fluent curves encircle the whole cinema on the top of the lobby. The overlapping three-layer roof is designed in the shape of a lotus blossom and paved with Italian marble in abstract patterns. The lobby and spacious lounge look splendid and graceful with artistic and cultural atmosphere.

- ☎ 021-63274260
- No. 216 Nanjing Rd. (w) 南京西路 216号
- Metro line No.1 and No.2 (People Square Station), Public buses 20, 37 and 921

YONGLE PALACE L15

永 乐 宫

◆ One of the first 4-star cinemas in Shanghai, it has 4 showrooms, featuring excellent original foreign films. It has been the principal cinema for showing films of the Shanghai International Film Festival. It enjoys a reputation of providing advanced facilities, good video visual effect and good service.

- ☎ 021-64312961
- No. 308 Anfu Rd. 安福路 308 号

- Metro line No.1 (Changshu Rd. Station), Metro line No.2 (Jiangsu Rd. Station), public buses 48 and 113

SHANGHAI INTERNATIONAL AUTOMOBILE CITY

上海国际汽车城

◆ The planned area of the automobile city is 4.8 sq.km., consisting of automobile transaction area, exhibition area, materials and accessories logistic area, service area for the metropolis and a tourist area of automobile culture. Once completed, sales headquarters and agencies of internationally renown automobile suppliers, and multi-national purchasing center will come to set up their offices here. Many brand speciality stores will also flock to this place. A network of automobile trade will reach every corner of the world. It will become an automobile trading market, an automobile hub in our country and even in the Asian-Pacific region.

021-59567725

No. 79 Moyu Rd., Anting, Shanghai
上海市安亭墨玉路 79 号

SHANGHAI INTERNATIONAL CAR RACE COURT

上海国际赛车场

◆ Located in Jiading District, northeast of Anting town, it neighbors world-renowned Shanghai International Automobile City. The F1 race tracks are in the shape of a huge Chinese character " 上 ", and are the most advanced and challenging tracks in the world. The stands are planned to hold about 200, 000 people, and there are 50,000 seats in the main and sub stands. The rest are temporary stands. The main building and other architectures occupy an area of 150, 000 sq.m., including the main and sub stands, race court command center, news center, residential areas of race teams and maitenance station. These constructions adopt the design concept of blending modern shape and Chinese traditional culture. Upon completion, the race court will add to the vigor and vitality of Shanghai.

* Phase I race area, with 2.5 sq.m. in area, and RMB2,645,000,000 in total investment, has been completed in March 2004, and has hosted 2004 China F1 Grand Prix. The reserved area of 2.5 sq.m. will be used for a new international multi-functional area with beautiful environment, convenient transportation and funtions of sports, leisure, entertainment and holiday. It is to built in accordance with F1 Grand Prix and automobile culture.

40 yuan (only groups with 10 people or more are accepted)

021-69569999

Northeast of Anting Town, Jiading District 上海市嘉定区安亭镇东北

BAOSTEEL

走进宝钢

◆ It is the largest and most modernized iron and steel complex established in new China. In 1997, the complex ranked at the top in its comprehensive strength among the 500 extra large enterprises in China and among the top 100 ones in Asia. Walking into the 18.9-sq.km. complex area you will be surprised to find yourself amidst the luxuriantly green ecological environ—ment. Baosteel is a national model unit in landscaping with 40% of its area covered in green. About a hundred deer roam about on the green lawns. Baosteel pursues the principle of "first human priority", pays attention to ecological and environmental protection and sustainable development.

* The towering blast furnaces, the blazing molten iron rushing out day and night, shooting high, spread a flush of gold like a waterfall under sunlight.

* Chairman Jiang Zemin inscribed for the group of sculptured oxen "Carrying forward thecause and forging into the future; Advance courageously".

* RECOMMENDED TOURS:

Tour A: Patriotism educational tour: Baosteel - Baoshan Martyrs' Cemetery - Linjiang Park - General Chen Huacheng Memorial Hall - Song Hu Anti-Japanese War Memorial Hall

Tour B: Baosteel leisurely tour: Baosteel - Baoshan Vegetable and Horticultural Field - Dakang Amusement Center

Tour C: Baosteel and Treasure Island tour: Baosteel - Changxing Island (boating in Reed Marshes, picking oranges in orchards and picking shells in shoals) - Hengsha Island

Tour D: Tour of cruising on Huangpu River and Enjoying the view of Baosteel: Baosteel - views on both banks of Huangpu River: buildings of architecture of the Middle Ages on the west bank and groups of high-rises, Oriental Pearl TV Tower and Jinmao Tower on the east bank) Baosteel Group International Travel Service (designated hosting company for tourists) 1534 Mudanjiang Rd telephone: 56109247, 56111462

* Baosteel industrial tour: There are the magnificent and imposing world-class blast furnaces that catch visitors' breath.

HENGSHAN ROAD LEISURE STREET M15
衡山路休闲街

◆ The 2.3-km-long Hengshan Road was first built in 1922 and enjoys a history of over 80 years. It has many remaining fine historic architectures and landscape.

* With the flourishing of Xujiahui commercial circle in recent years, Hengshan Rd. combines business and tourism, emphasizing on various cuisines, bars, entertainment and gymnasium. Some clothes shops and fine arts stores are developped. The street is developped into an European-style leisure street in new Shanghai, with unique environment, corporate culture and featured business, providing featured services. Scores of amusement places line up the 2.3-km-long street, making the latter a famous entertainment and leisure street in Shanghai. The greening landscape along the two sides of Hengshan Rd. is of unique charm—over 500 French parasol trees are luxuriant and towering. It boasts one of the oldest and best-reserved road greening landscapes.

Metro line No.1 (Hengshan Rd Station), public buses 15 and 93

* The apartments and villas on Hengshan Rd. are of various styles—Spanish, British, country, immitation classic, which deserve the name: museum of world architectures. Among them the most famous ones are Hengshan Hotel, (Bikadi Apartment), West Lake Apartment (Washington Apartment), etc. The Community Church, built in 1925, is of bright and harmonious hue strong atmosphere of British church and religious culture.

＊ When night falls, fashionable youngsters come here for rest and relaxation by playing cards,chess and bowling, chatting, listening to music, disco dancing, etc. The place is full of vigor and vitality.

XINTIANDI

新 天 地

See p38-39

021-63112288

lane 181, Taichang Rd. 太仓路181弄

Metro line No.1 (Huangpi Rd. (S) Station) pulbic buses 42, 926 and 911

YUNNAN ROAD (S), A STREET OF SNACK BARS K17

云南南路美食街

Built in the 1860s and completed in the 1870s, the 1,261-m-long Yunnan Road starts from Huaihai Road (E), ends at Zhifu Road (E), and passes of South, Middle, and North Yunnan Road. The street of delicacies is the section from Jinling Road (E) to Yan'an Road (E).

Jinling Rd. corner of Yunnan Rd.
金陵东路、云南南路口

Public buses 26, 18, 71

* There are the famous Xiaoshaoxing Chicken Restaurant and Fusheng Roast Goose Restaurant in the southern end of the street. And in the northern end there are the 24-hour Xiang-manlou Snack Restaurant and the Changan 108-flavored "jiaozi" Restaurant. Besides, the street also boasts the Jinyun Shrimp Noodle Restaurant, the Little Jinling Salted Duck Restaurant, the Xuandelai New Year Cake and Pork Rib Restaurant, and the Nanxiang Steamed-Dumpling Restaurant.

ZHAPU ROAD, A STREET OF GOURMET FOOD J18

乍浦路美食街

◆ The street of delicacies started in the middle of 1980s and was developed in the early 1990s. It is a non-state-owned business formed by different kinds of ownership. It is an expression of the Chinese culture of food, wine and dishes, representing the essence of our eight styles of cuisine, consisting mainly of the Cantonese, Sichuan, Yangzhou, Jiangsu, Zhejiang and Shanghai specialties. It offers round-the-clock service and superb culinary skill, special cultural decorations and flexible management. The homely food there is well-known in whole Shanghai and as far as in the southeast Asia.

Zhapu Rd., corner of Haining Rd.
海宁路、乍浦路口

Public buses 19, 14 and 20

HUANGHE ROAD, A STREET OF GOURMET FOOD K17

黄河路美食街

◆ Originally, Huanghe Road was a small street with a history of over 100 years.

In this more than 300-m-long street there are about 60 restaurants with distinctive specialties. 17 out of 60 are private restaurants. There are large ones like the Gongdelin, Great Hong Kong, the Little, Dafuhao Restaurants, Dynasty Amusement City, Laitianhua and Yindu Seafood Restaurants.

Near Nanjing Road, Huanghe Road boasts a number of restaurants and a favorable location, adding much to the prosperity of the bustling city.

Huanghe Rd. 黄河路

Metro line No.1 and No.2 (People's Square Station), Public buses 20, 21 and 37

FUZHOU ROAD CULTURAL STREET K17
福州路文化街

◆ On the cultural street gather over 30 different bookstores and stationery shops, such as Shanghai Bookmall, China Science and Technology Bookstore, Foreign Languages Bookstore, as well as a number of stationery shops and business departments of publishing houses. It is well-known in the whole country as "a cultural street".

Fuzhou Rd. 福州路

Metro line No.1 & No.2 (People Square Station) Public buses 17, 49 and 123

DONGTAI ROAD ANTIQUE STREET L17
东台路古玩街

◆ Dongtai Road Antique Street is a featured business street. In over 200 stalls and over 40 shops old arts and crafts of porcelain, jade-ware, copperware, wood-ware, calligraphy and paintings, "four treasures of the study" (brush, ink, ink-stone and paper) and miscellaneous articles are sold. The market is quite popular in the country and abroad, attracting many working staff, different consuls and tourists from home and abroad.

Dongtai Rd., corner of Shunchang Rd.
顺昌路、东台路口

Public buses 17, 18 and 23

TAIKANG ROAD ARTS STREET M17

泰康路艺术街

◆ It is named by artists as "a warehouse of arts". Walking along Taikang Road you will feel the cultural atmosphere of old Shanghai culture and its marketplace heritage. Here you will find a great variety of traditional arts and crafts and embroideries.

Taikang Rd., corner of Ruijing Rd.
瑞金一路、泰康路口

Public buses 41, 24, 128 and 43

✻ Letian Pottery Bar: In the bar there are masterpieces by artists imbued with their creative ideas and exquisite skills. There are all kinds of tools for making pottery.

✻ Baby brides: There are different kinds of traditional, antique artistic and practical articles for weddings of individual feature, such as candy boxes, wedding invitation cards, glassware, etc. Customers may also order artistic sculptures of wedding.

Gourmet

Shanghai Food

Shanghai Old Restaurant
Add: No. 242 Fuyou Rd.
Tel: 63111777

Dexinguan Restaurant
Add: No. 29 Dongmen Rd.
Tel: 63281426

Lvbolang Restaurant
Add: No. 115 Yuyuan Rd.
Tel: 63280602

Old Zhengxin Restaurant
Add: No. 556 Fuzhou Rd.
Tel: 63515496

Hangzhou Food

New Kaiyuan Restaurant
Add: No. 560 Xujiahui Rd.
Tel: 64668866

Zhangsheng Restaurant
Add: Yitaili Building, No. 446 Zaojiabang Rd.
Tel: 64455777

West Lake Restaurant
Add: No. 1805 Sichuan Rd. (N)
Tel: 56662415

Ningbo Food

Harvest Restaurant
Add: No. 93 Caobao Rd.
Tel: 54977770

Ningbo Family
Add: in Jinjiang Hotel, No. 691 Jianguo Rd. (W)
Tel: 64155688

Sichuan Food

Romance of Sichuan
Add: 2nd floor of Guangfa Bank Building, No. 555 Xujiahui Rd.
Tel: 63901436

Baguo Buyi
Add: No. 1676 Hongqiao Rd.
Tel: 62706668

Legend of Sichuan
Add: No. 1440 Hongqiao Rd.
Tel: 62088260

Yangzhou Food

Meilongzhen Restaurant
Add: No. 22, lane 1081, Nanjing Rd. (W)
Tel: 62566705

Yangzhou Restaurant
Add: No. 31 Sinan Rd.
Tel: 53832023

Lvyangcun Restaurant
Add: No. 763 Nanjing Rd. (W)
Tel: 62584422

Cantonese Food

Tan's Official Residence Restaurant
Add: 4th floor, No. 3190 Yan'an Rd. (W)
Tel: 64658080

Xinghualou Restaurant
Add: No. 343 Fuzhou Rd.
Tel: 63553777

Sunya Cantonese Restaurant
Add: No. 719 Naning Rd. (E)
Tel: 63517788

Chaozhou Food

Boduoxin Restaurant
Add: No. 4, lane 9 Baoqing Rd.
Tel: 64745301

Meiyuehua Restaurant
Add: No. 222 Zaojiabang Rd.
Tel: 64667777

Xiang Food

Spring of Dongting Lake Restaurant
Add: No. 50 Puhuitang Rd.
Tel: 64395288

Dripping Water Cave
Add: 2nd floor 56, Maoming Rd. (S)
Tel: 62532689

Beijing Food

Quanjude Roast Duck Restaurant
Add: No. 547 Tianmu Rd. (W)
Tel: 63538558

Yanyunlou Restaurant
Add: No. 755 Nanjing Rd. (E)
Tel: 63609698

Food in Northeast China

Beidahuang Bu Liao Qing Restaurant
Add: No. 1515 Zhongshan Rd. (E2)
Tel: 65559191-0366

Great Qinghua
Add: No. 466 Changde Rd.
Tel: 62899999

Yunnan Food

Daijiacun Restaurant
Add: No. 159 Aomen Rd.
Tel: 62271465

Yunan Delicacy Garden
Add: No. 568 Xujiahui Rd.
Tel: 64673038

Anhui Food

Dafugui Restaurant
Add: No. 1409 Zhonghua Rd.
Tel: 63770322

Shandong Food

Huamei Pavilion
Add: 2nd floor of Qilu Wanyi Hotel, No. 838 Dongfang Rd.
Tel: 68867188

CHINESE FOOD STYLE SERIES 各式菜系一览

Vegetable Dishes

Gongdelin Vegetarian Restaurants
Add: No. 455 Nanjing Rd. (W)
Tel:63270218

Jujube Tree
Add: Shanghai Palace, No. 77 Songshan Rd.
Tel: 63848000

Juelin Vegetable Restaurants
Add: No. 250 Jinling Rd. (E)
Tel: 63260115

Hot Pot

Hong Changxing Moutton Restaurant
Add: No. 288 Guangxi Rd. (N)
Tel: 63529700

Dong Laishun Restaurant
Add: No. 9 Sinan Rd.
Tel: 53064407

Laifulou Restaurant
Add: 2nd floor, No. 10 Hengshan Rd.
Tel: 64746545

Noodles and Snacks

Nanxiang Steamed Bread Restaurant
Add: No. 85 Yuyuan Rd.
Tel: 63265265

Wangjiasha Snacks
Add: No. 805 Nanjing Rd. (W)
Tel: 62170625

Shendacheng Snacks
Add: No. 636 Nanjing Rd. (E)
Tel: 63225615

Argentine Food

Argentine Roast Restaurant
Add: No. 299 Xianxia Rd.
Tel: 62351828

Brazilian Food

Latin Restaurant
Add: 18, lane, No. 181 Taichang Rd.
Tel: 64722718

Dajiama Brizilian Roast Meat
Add: 18th floor, Meiluo City, No. 1111 Zhaojiabang Rd.
Tel: 64267057

German Food

Baolaina Restaurant
Add: No. 150 Fenyang Rd.
Tel: 64745700

French Food

Axiangdi
Add: No. 16 Gaolan Rd.
Tel: 53061230

Lemeisong
Add: 123 lane, No. 181 Taichang Rd.
Tel: 33071010

Korean Food

Gaoli Restaurant
Add: New building of Donghu Hotel, No. 7 Donghu Rd.
Tel: 64158158*77400

Hanlin BBQ
Add: 1st floor, Peace Square, No. 18 Shuicheng Rd.
Tel: 62951204

American Food

Rib Restaurant
Add: No. 1 Yueyang Rd.s
Tel: 64332969

Malong American Cafe
Add: No. 555 Tongren Rd.
Tel: 62472400

Mexican Restaurant
Add: 2nd floor, No. 176 Maoming Rd. (S)
Tel: 64337459

Japanese Food

Dajianghu
Add: No. 30 Donghu Rd.
Tel: 54035877

Haizhixing Japanese Food Restaurant
Add: No. 402 Shaanxi Rd. (S)
Tel: 64453406

Yitengjia
Add: No. 24 Ruiin, No.2 Rd.
Tel: 64730758

Thai Food

Jinxiangyuan Thai Restaurant
Add: 2nd floor, Nanxinya, No. 700 Jiujiang Rd.
Tel: 63501163

Tiantai
Add: C building, No. 5 Dongping Rd.
Tel: 64459551

Italian Food

Languifang
Add: Fuxing Park, No. 2 Gaolan Rd.
Tel: 53832328

Luna
Add: 16 lane, No. 181 Taichang Rd.
Tel: 63361717

Indian Food

Indian Restaurant
Add: No. 572 Yongjia Rd.
Tel: 64731517

Jinjin Carrie
Add: No. 151 Wanping Rd. (S)
Tel: 64277738

Vietnamese Food

Los Angles Vietamese Food
Add: No. 781 Huangjincheng Rd.
Tel: 62097669

酒吧、俱乐部、咖啡吧、茶坊一览 BARS, CLUBS, CAFES AND TEAHOUSES

TEAHOUSE

Classic Rose Garden
1th floor of Zhengda Plaza, 168 Lujiazui Rd. (W)
021-50473012

Yihe Teahouse
158 Huanyuan shiqiao Rd.
021-58777797

Rose Garden (Ganghui branch)
166 Ganghui Square, 1 Hongqiao Rd.
021-64078840

Gu Garden
1315 Fuxing Rd. (M)
021-64454625

Hanyuan Book House
27 Shaoxing Rd.
021-64732526

Forest of Flowers Teahouse
1) 1686 Huashan Rd.
021-62803269
2) 2 Weifang Rd.
021-58888758
3) 1248 Changde Rd.
021-62773801
4) 251Dalian Rd. (W)
021-65229630
5) 102, 121 Wanting Rd.
021-54378495

Tangyun Teahouse
1)199 Hengshan Rd.
021-34060126
2) 3-4 floor Xianshi Leisure Harbor, 479, Nanjing Rd. (E)
021-63220038

Qingtengge Teahouse
1) 414 Zhaojiabang Rd.
021-64371972
2) 528 Anlong Rd.
021-62622850
3) 25 Changyi Rd.
021-68870428
4) 1111 Yan'an Rd. (M)
021-62491616

Huifengtang Teahouse
2424 Xietu Rd.
021-64877449

Jiangnan Tea Bar
In Quyang Park, 880 Zhongshan Rd. (N1)
021-65424017

Yaqu Teahouse (Dongfang branch)
Opposite Holiday Inn 918 Dongfang Rd.
021-68767305

Jishanyuan Vegetable Dishes Teahouse
627 Guangyuan Rd. (W)
021-64078285

Taihe Teahouse
569 Pudong Avenue
021-68877880

Diagonal Black Teahouse
2091 Sichuan Rd. (N)
021-56967496

CAFE

Red Dot
In Riverside Park on Fudu section of Riverside Promenade
021-58871818

The Coffee Beanery
1) 9 Qinghai Rd.
021-62539192
2) Grand Theatre Ticket Office Huangpi Rd. (N)
021-63721088
3) 88th floor, Jinmao Tower, 88 Century Boulevard
021-50471804
4) Rm 101, 777 lane Biyun Rd.
021-50305688
5) Rm 101, 1181Xiuyan Rd.
021-68195758
6) Hall E2, Shanghai New Exposition Center 2345 Longyang Rd.
021-28906783

I'Aroma
4 Jianguo Rd. (M)
021-54562077

Delifrance
1st floor of Zhonghuan Square, 381 Huaihai Rd. (M)
021-53825171

Coffee Bean&Tea Leaf
1) 10th building, north of Xintiandi Square, lane 181 Taichang Rd.
021-63874248
2) Rm B, 1st floor, JInling Haixin building, 666 Fuzhou Rd.
021-63917971
3) 140 Hongqiao Shanghai City, 100 Zunyi Rd.
021-62371458

Boonna Cafe
88 Xinle Rd.
021-54046676

CoffeeLox
1) 1st floor of Paris Spring Hotel, 1525 Dingxi Rd.
021-62525394
2) 1st floor, 75 Loushanguan Rd.
021-32231478
3) 1st floor of Xinluda Department Store 1988 Huashan Rd.
021-54070785
3) 1st floor of Zhongxin Department Store, 718 Caoxi Rd. (N)
021-64387238
4) Rm B, 40 Jinling Rd. (W)
021-63849899

Madrid
146 Maoming Rd. (S)
021-64721531

Tixiang Cafe
263 Wanping Rd. (S)
021-64261982

Living Quarters
91 Changle Rd.
021-53832936

Cafe Transat
West block of Shengjie Aparment, 8 Jinan Rd.
021-53828370

Vienna Cafe
2nd Building, 25 Shaoxing Rd.
021-64452131

Keven Cafe Restaurant
525 Hengshan Rd.
021-64335564

Delifrance
1) No. 1 business building in Raffles City, 268 Xizang Rd. (M)
021-63403916
2) 1st floor of Zhonghuan Square , 381 Huaihai Rd. (M)
021-53825171

Yuandao Cafe
2218 Sichuan Rd. (N)
021-65873775

Old Film Cafe
123 Duolun Rd.
021-56964763

Tima Harbour
1) 134-137 street of delicacies, Hongqiao and Shanghai City, 100 Zunyi Rd.
021-62371063
2) 11 Zhenning Rd.
021-62258684

Jinmao Grand Hyatt Cafe
54th floor of The Jinmao Grand Hyatt Hotel, 88 Century Boulevard
021-50491234

Siji Cafe
1st floor of Siji Hotel, 500 Weihai Rd.
021-62568888

Fuhao Dongya Cafe
1st floor of Fuhao Dongya Hotel, 800 Linling Rd.
021-64266888-8322

Marriott
38th floor of JW Marriott Hotel, Tomorrow Square, 399 Nanjing Rd. (W)
021-53594969

Mageboluo Cafe
186 Xinhua Rd.
021-62814448

Haosheng Cafe
1st floor of Guxiang Hotel, 595 Jiujiang Rd.
021-33134888

Guidu Cafe
1st floor of International Guidu Hotel, 65 yan'an Rd. (W)
021-62481688

Xiangzhang Garden Cafe
1st floor of Xingguo Hotel, 78 Xingguo Rd.
021-62129998

Deck Cafe
4th floor of Haishen Funuote Hotel, 728 Pudong Avenue
021-50366666

Renaissance Cafe
1st floor of Yangtze Renaissance Hotel, 2099 Yan'an Rd. (W)
021-62750000

Art Deco
No 3 building, Ruijin Hotel, 118 No. 2Ruijing Rd.
021-64725222

Venus Cafe
1st floor Sino Petrol Hotel,969 Dongfang Rd.
021-68758888-3807

Marriott Cafe (Hongqiao)
1st floor of Marriott Hongqiao Hotel, 2270 Hongqiao Rd.
021-62376000

Cafe on 2nd floor of Wangbaohe
2nd floor of Wangbaohe Hotel, 555 Jiujiang Rd.
021-53965000

Angel Cafe
3rd floor of Holiday Inn, 585 Hengfeng Rd.
021-63538008-5841

Crown Cafe
Silver Star Crown Hotel, 400 Fanyu Rd.
021-62808888

Denny Cafe
156 Ganghui Square, 1 Hongqiao Rd.
021-64070047

Palm Island Cafe
1F Hongqiao Hotel, 1591 Hongqiao Rd.
021-62198855

BAR / CLUB

The Door
3rd floor,1468 Hongqiao Rd.
021-62953737

Colours
No 11 Building, Ruijin Hotel, 118 No. 2 Ruijin Rd.
021-54665577

Paradise
1F, Building No 5, Xintiandi Square, lane 123 Xingye Rd.
021-63365860

Laodifang
2B building, 22, lane 181 Xingye Rd.
021-63365383

O' Malley's Irish Pub
42 Taojiang Rd
021-64370667

FACE
4th floor of Ruijin Hotel , 118 No. 2 Ruijin Rd.
021-64664328

Baoliana Restaurant
1) Northern Xintiandi Square, lane 181 Taichang Rd.
021-63203935
2) 150 Fenyang rd
021-64745700
3) Central Green Belt in Pudong, facing the Huangpu River(diagonnaly oppositeShangri-la)
021-68883935

CJW
1) 1st floor of No. 2 building, lane 123 Xingye Rd., Xintiandi
021-63856677
2) 50th floor Bund Center, 222 Yan'an Rd. (E)
021-63391777

Malong American Bar
255 Tongren Rd.
021-62472400

M-BOX
3rd floor, 1 Baoqing Rd.
021-64678777

JW Marriott Lounge
40th floor of JW Marriot Hotel, Tomorrow Square, 399 Nanjing Rd (W)
021-53594969

DR
Unit 4 of No 15 building, north Xintiandi Square, lane 181 Taichang Rd.
021-63110358

Piano Bar
53th floor of Grand Hyatt Hotel, 88 Century Avenue
021-50491234

Azul&Viva
18 Dongping Rd.
021-64331172

Kathleen's 5
5th floor of Shanghai Art Museum, 325 Nanjing Rd. (W)
021-63272221

Nine Sky Bar
87th floor of Jinmao Grand Hyatt Hotel, 88 Century Avenue
021-50491234-8787

1931 Pub
112 Maoming Rd. (S)
021-64725264

Arch
439 Wukang Rd.
021-64660807

Mesa&Manifesto
748 Julu Rd.
021-62899108

Sasha's
11 Dongping Rd.
021-64746628

kommune
quadrangle dwelling, 7 lane 210 Taikang Rd.
021-64662416

New Heights
7th floor,3 bund, 3 Zhongshan Rd. (E1)
021-63210909

Mint Club
2nd floor, 333 Tongren Rd.
021-62479666

BARS, CLUBS, CAFES AND TEAHOUSES 酒吧、俱乐部、咖啡吧、茶坊一览

Always Cafe
1528 Nanjing Rd. (W)
021-62478333

Pujin
3rd floor of Jinmao Grand Hyatt Hotel, 88 Century Avenue
021-50491234

Third Degree
7th floor, 3 Bund, 3 Zhongshan Rd. (E1)
021-63210909

Tuberrose
3rd floor, Garden Hotel, 58 Maoming Rd. (S)
021-64151111-5217

Guandii
Fuxing Park, 2 Gaolan Rd.
021-33080726

Bar Rouge
7th floor, 18 Bund, 18 Zhongshan Rd. (E1)
021-63391199

WINDOWS
1)2nd floor, Yimei, Jiang'an Temple, 1333 Nanjing Rd. (W)
021-32140351
2)186 Maoming Rd. (S)
021-62475648
3)3rd floor, 681 Huaihai Rd. (M)
021-53827757

MURAL Bar & Restaurant
Basement,697 Yongjia Rd.
021-64335023

Le Pub 505
2nd floor of Sofitel Hyland Hotel, 505 Nanjing Rd. (E)
021-63515888

Cotton Club
1428 Huaihai Rd. (M)
021-64377110

ViP Room
In A-4 Jing'an Temple Culture Hall, 459 Wulumuqi Rd. (N)
021-62488898

Blues&Jazz
158 Maoming Rd. (S)
021-64375270

Bund Beer Club
11 Hankou Rd.
021-63218034

BATS
1st floor of Shangri-la,33 Fucheng Rd.
021-68828888

Senses Wine Lounge
515 Jianguo Rd. (W)
021-54921655

Green House
135 Yili Rd.
021-62708889

Baby Face
1)180 Maoming Rd. (S)
021-64452330
2)Shanghai Square,138 Huaihai Rd (M)

CHEG SIMONE
207 Maoming Rd. (S)
021-64159701

Dragon Club
156 Fenyang Rd.
021-54044592

Tang Hui
13 Xingfu Rd.
021-62815646

New Space
2nd floor of Nine Hundred Century Food City, 50 Wanhangdu Rd.
021-62583466

Cru Bar
1st floor 2099 Renasissence Yangtze Shanghai Hotel
Yan'an Rd. (W)
021-62750000-2168

Frog Bar
3208 Hongmei Rd.
021-64010139

LUNA
Sasson Hair College, 15 lane 169 Taichang Rd.
021-63361717

42 A MUSIC CLUB
42, No. 2 Ruijin Rd.
021-64726899

Blue Frog
1) 207 Maoming Rd. (S)
021-64456634
2) 86 Tongren Rd.
021-62470320
3) Hongmei Leisure Street, lane 3338 Hongmei Rd.
021-54225119
4) in gymnasium, 633 Biyun Rd.
021-50306426

I'm Shanghainese
168 Maoming Rd. (S)
021-64152188

Judy's Too
1) 176 Maoming Rd. (S)
021-64731417
2) 1st floor of 78-80 Tongren Rd.
021-62893715

Hongfan Music Restaurant
10A Hengshan Rd.
021-64746828

Armanni Club
Basement, Shanghai Film City, 160 Xinhua Rd.
021-62806628

Huanxisha
Consulate Square, 4-8 Hengshan Rd.
021-54654748

JA Lounge Bar
Jing'an Park, 1649 Nanjing Rd. (W)
021-62487034

PINK 8
551 Caoxi Rd. (N)
021-64696823

SoHo
1) Unit 5, 3 lane 181 Taichang Rd
021-33071000
2) 35 Sinan Rd.
021-53831030

Yesterday, Today, Tomorrow
183 lane 1038, Huashan Rd.
021-62402588

Star East
17th Building, North Xintiandi, 181 Taichang Rd.
021-63114991

Bourbon Street
191 Hengshan Rd.
021-64737911

Beni (Benny's Bar)
705 Yongjia Rd.
021-64335964

Shanghai Fans
unit 04, 1st Building, Xintiandi, 119 Madang Rd.
021-53833182

M-FACTORY
170 Maoming Rd. (S)
021-64151088

Rojam
4th floor of Hongkong Square, 283 Huaihai Rd. (M)
021-63907181

Wendy's
141 Maoming Rd. (S)
021-64732849

Bailan American-style Mexico Bar
895 Julu Rd.
021-64667788-8003

Original Taste
Rm 102, 20 lane 777 Biyun Rd.
021-50304228

Long Bar
2nd floor of Shanghai Commercial City, 1376, Nanjing Rd. (W)
021-62798268

Captainbar
6th floor of 37, Fuzhou Rd.
021-63237869

Daming Bar and Restaurant with River View
19th floor of Xingyuan Hotel, 1191 Dongdaming Rd.
021-65373399

Papa's Bierstube
17 Hongmei Leisure Street, lane 3338 Hongmei Rd.
021-64658880

Bundi Bar
281 Hengshan Rd.
021-64334183

Black Box Bar
2069 Siping Rd.
021-55671001

Canna Sightseeing Restaurant
Top floor of Canna Hotel, 7 Yan'an Rd. (E)
021-63300022-188

T&B
138 Fenyang Rd.
021-54656579

Jazz 37 Bar
37th floor of Four Season Hotel Shanghai, 500 Weihai Rd.
021-62568888-1750

JZ Club
46 Fuxing Rd. (W)
021-64310269

Old House Inn
16, lane 351 Huashan Rd.
021-62488020

Lijia Bar
2nd floor of Portman Hotel, 1376 Nanjing Rd. (W)
021-62798888

Sky Dome Bar
New World Lisheng Hotel, 88 Nanjing Rd. (W)
021-63599999

Two Doors Resaurant-Third Degree Bar
9 Hongmei Rd Leisure Street, lane 3338 Hongmei Rd.
021-64659699

SPORTS MANIA
3rd floor of 458 Tianyaoqiao Rd.
021-54256285

Garden Hotel Lobby Bar
1st floor of Garden Hotel, 58 Maoming Rd. (S)
021-64151111

Mokalika
64 Wulumuqi Rd.s (S)
021-54658288

Next
2nd floor of 575 Caoxi Rd. (N)
021-64693277

Nizang Garden Restaurant and Bar
427 B, Dongyuansicun, Dongchang Rd.
021-58772262

Cafe and Bar
180 Shanghai Stadium Rd.
021-28772716

Pandora Bar
680 Xianxia Rd.
021-62612465

Tsingdao Bar
2365 Sichuan Rd. (N)
021-56965655

Stone Bar
No 2 building, Hongqiao Guesthouse, 1591 Hongqiao Rd.
021-62198855

Roof Garden Night Shanghai Bar
11 Open air Garden, North Building of Peace Hotel, 20 Nanjing Rd. (E)
021-63216888

West Side
237 Hengshan Rd.
021-64724327

Hilton Bar
39th floor, Hilton Hotel, 250 Huashan Rd.
021-62480000

Peace Restaurant and Bar
222 Zaojiabang Rd.
021-54644477

ARK
15 north Xintiandi Square, lane 181 Taichang Rd.
021-63268008

Nightcat club
458 Tianyaoqiao Rd.
021-64281899

Hard Rock
260 Zhengtong Rd.
021-65119178

Lounge Bar
1st floor of Ruiji Hongta Hotel, 889 Dongfang Rd.
021-50504567

Main shopping streets and

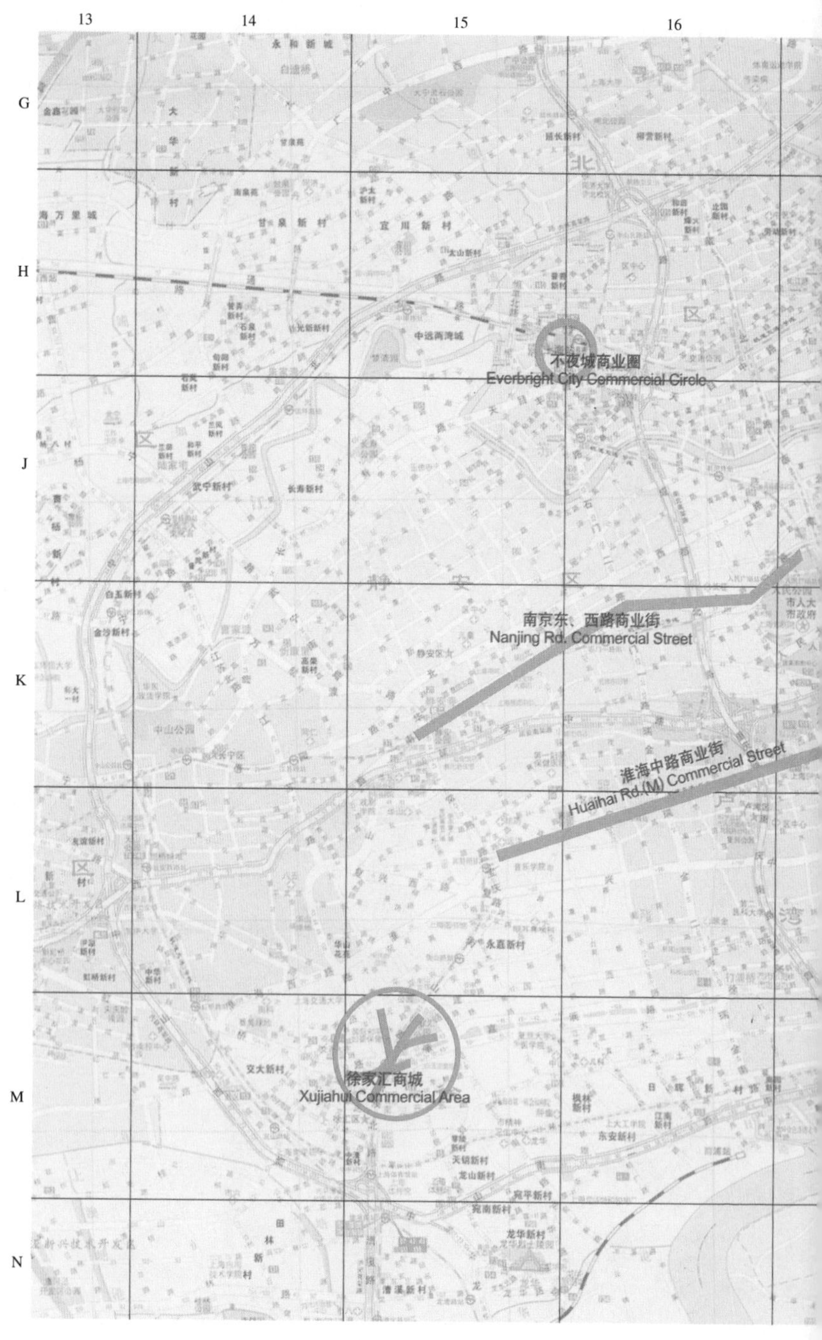

shopping malls of Shanghai 上海主要商街、商城

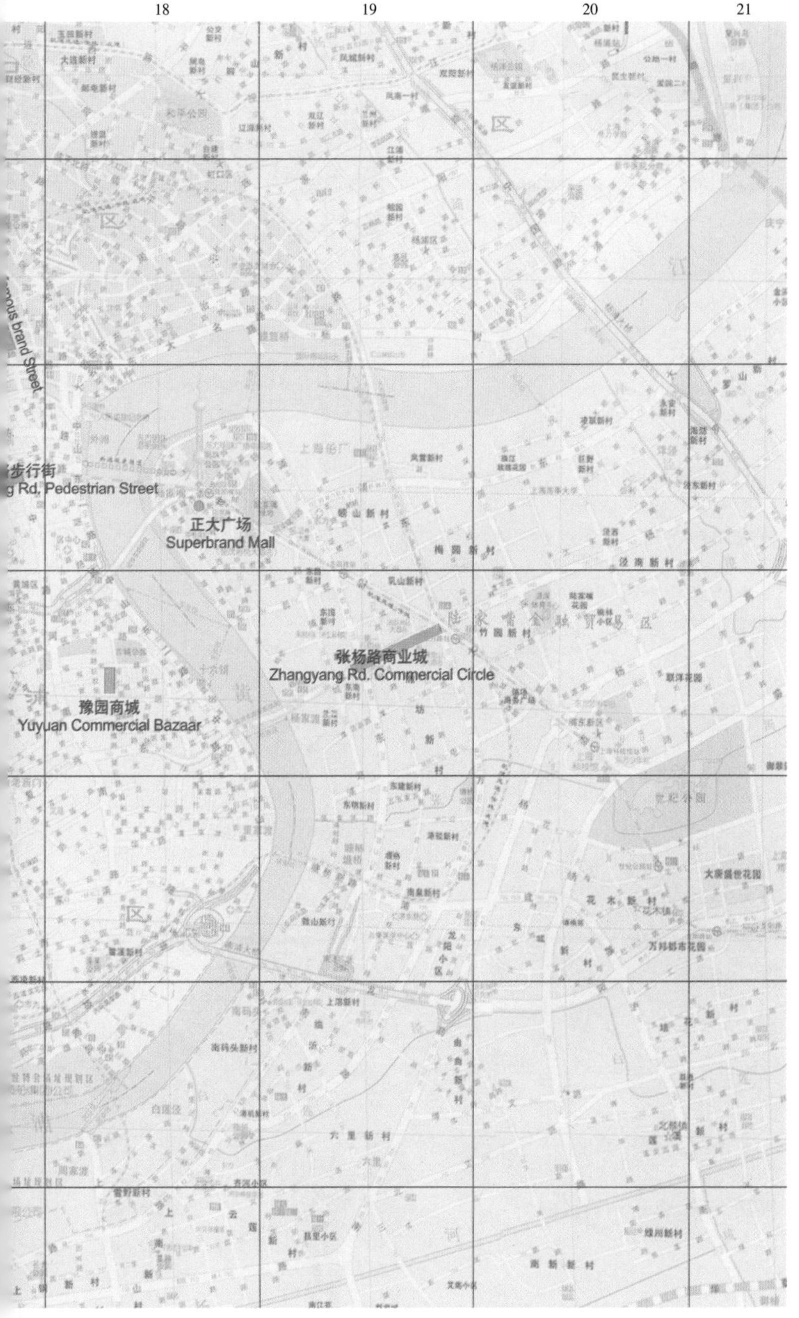

NANJING ROAD COMMERCIAL STREET K16

南京东、西路商业街

◆ In the 20th century, along with the setting up of the world-famous department stores of the "Wing On", "Sincere", "Sun Sun" and "Dai Sun", businessmen of all trades flocked to this piece of precious land, Nanjing Road, the well-known "No.1 Commercial Street in China", to set up their own stores. Thus, Nanjing Road soon became "a street of prosperity, glaring with lights and glamour", the most prosperous and bustling street in Shanghai.

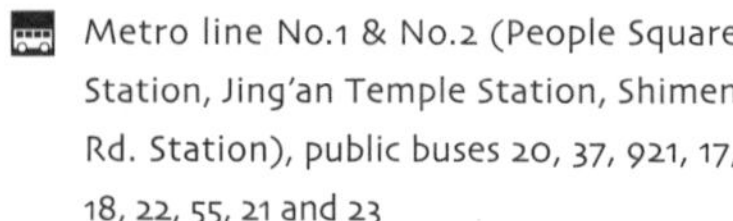
Metro line No.1 & No.2 (People Square Station, Jing'an Temple Station, Shimen Rd. Station), public buses 20, 37, 921, 17, 18, 22, 55, 21 and 23

* After Liberation, Nanjing Road has been renovated several times and become the principal commercial street in Shanghai, with rows of shops around 600 of different trades on both sides. It is, indeed, the "No.1 Commercial Street" in Shanghai.

* There are the old-brand stores and restaurants still booming with business and new department stores and malls emerging one after another, like the New World, the Landmark Square, Manhatten Plaza, Hongxiang and Sincere Co. Nanjing Rd. (E). And on Nanjing Rd. (W) there are Meilongzhen Plaza, Citic Square and Plaza 66, mainly dealing in super-fine and high-grade consumer goods and boasting the favorites of Shanghai modern office ladies.

关爱生命与健康

银树
雅戈尔

✻ One feature of Nanjing Road is that it still keeps the tradition of being "No.1 Commercial Street in China", playing the leading role in commerce in the country. People can find a great variety of commodities from all places in the country and even from southeast Asia and abroad. There are commodities various in grades that meet the needs of customers of different social strata.

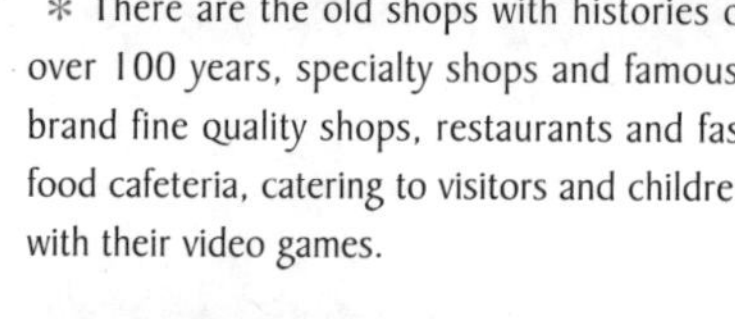

✻ There are the old shops with histories of over 100 years, specialty shops and famous-brand fine quality shops, restaurants and fast food cafeteria, catering to visitors and children with their video games.

WORLD
向阳世界
SUBWAY

HUAIHAI ROAD (M), COMMERCIAL STREET L16

淮海中路商业街

◆ Formerly known as Avenue Joffre, the 6-km-long Huaihai Road, a shopping street of elegance and prosperity, enjoys the same prosperity as Nanjing Road. It is a counterpart in Shanghai to Avenue des Champs Elysees in Paris, the Fifth Avenue in New York, the Sinza in Tokyo and Wujie Road in Singapore.

Metro line No.1 (Huangpi Rd. (S) and Shanxi Rd. (S) Stations), public buses 42, 926, 24, 126 and 911

* Huaihai Road collects the finest quality goods in the world. Paris Spring, Maison Mode and Huating Isetan supply the top quality brands of the world. Shanghai, therefore, is a place that offers world's top-grade commodities.

* The buildings on both sides of Huaihai Road are modernized. The shops look elegant and elitist in Chinese, European or American classic or up-to-date European, and trans-century styles. Both the exterior decorations and interior layout of the buildings present a strong metropolitan cultural flavor.

* There are around 400 shops with modernized feature on Huaihai Road. The most prosperous section of the street is the 2.2-km-long section from Shanxi Road to Xizang Road. The transformation of Huaihai Road and the construction of the subway started simultaneously. The remolding started with a high level, thus making the street match with the position of Shanghai as a world metropolis.

太平洋百货

L'ORÉAL
PARIS

YANDANG ROAD LEISURELY WALKWAY K16

雁荡路休闲街

♦ Located in northern Luwan District, the 542.5-m-long walkway runs from Huaihai Road (M) to Fuxing Park Avenue, crossing Xing'an Rd and Nanchang Rd. It is a round-the-clock walkway with cafes, bars, restaurants, amusement centers and beauty parlors.

Yandang Rd. 雁荡路

Metro line No.1 (Huangpi Rd (S) Station, Shaanxi Rd (S) Station), Public buses 926, 02, 911 and 920

* There are Italian pizza huts, German sports chocolates, Singaporean cafes, Japanese fast food in varied specialty and flavor.

* There is healthcare drinks from Hong Kong, egg tarts from Macao, teas and rice cakes from Taiwan that meet the taste of visitors.

* There are also Chinese restaurants with their specialty cuisines, such as Sichuan food, noodles, etc. They enjoy far-flung fame both at home and abroad.

FORMER SITE OF THE FIRST NATIONAL CONGRESS OF THE COMMUNIST PARTY OF CHINA K17

"中共"一大会址

◆ Located on Xingye Road, it is a typical residence of wood-and-brick "shikumen" structure in the 1920s of Shanghai. It is now a key cultural relic under state protection. The first national congress of the Chinese Communist Party was held here.

- am: 8:30 pm: 13:15
- am: 11:00 pm: 16:00
- 3 yuan
- 021-53832171-111
- No. 76 Xingye Rd. 兴业路 76 号
- Metro line No.1 (Huangpi Rd. (S) Station), Public buses 109, 24 and 17
- 60 minutes

* The 200-sq.m. hall on the first floor is a lecture hall equipped with audio video facilities.

* On the second floor there is the newly established exhibition hall of "Historical Relics of the Founding of the Communist Party of China". Displayed in the 450-sq.m. rooms (4 times as the original size) are nearly 100 pieces of cultural relics such as precious photos of the delegates to the congress, cultural relics, documents and other photos. There is a wax figure exhibition, showing the actual historical scene of this great event.

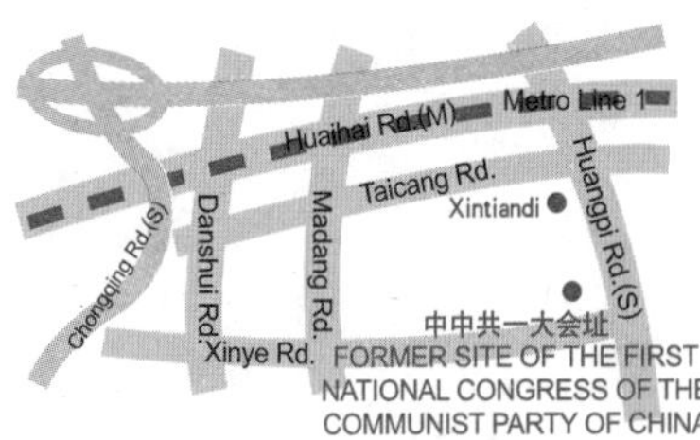

THE GREEN LAND AROUND TAIPING BRIDGE K17

太平桥绿地

- Huangpi Rd., (S), corner of Zizhong Rd. 黄陂南路、自忠路口
- Metro line No.1, public buses 109 and 43

◆ Taipingqiao green belt stretches in three directions: from Ji'an Road to Huangpi Road (N) in the east, to Zizhong Road in the south, and to Hubin Road in the north. Among the modernized high-rise complex on Huaihai Rd, such a large tract of luxuriant green land encircles a placid lake with banks winding in a beautiful arc shape. Visitors can take a leisurely walk along the pebble path around the lake while enjoying the freshness of the green belt and appreciate the beautiful scenery.

XUJIAHUI COMMERCIAL AREA M15

徐家汇商业城

◆ Located in southwest Shanghai, Xujiahui Commercial Area occupies an area of 1.2 sq. km. with Xujiahui Square as the center and 500,000 sq.m floor space of business establishments. There are such famous malls as Oriental Shopping Center, Pacific Department Store, Shanghai No.6 Department Store, Zhongxing Department Store, Huilian Commercial Building, Bainaohui Computer Center, Daqian Delicacies Restaurant, Jianguo Hotel and Huating Hotel, offering services for shopping, amusement, catering and supplying goods of different grades to meet the needs of different social strata. It is now a modern commercial hot spot.

Metro line No.1 (Xujiahui Station) Public buses 15, 43, 44, 56 and 42

GRAND GATEWAY M15

港 汇 广 场

◆ Located at the intersection of Huashan Road and Hongqiao Road and in the center of Xujiahui commercial area, it is a symbolic building in Shanghai, with magnificent architecture, harmonious layout and elegant style. It has been listed by Shanghai People's Government as the site for receiving foreign guests. The plaza offers services for shopping, catering, amusement, and tourism in a relaxed environment and pleasant atmosphere.

ORIENTAL SHOPPING CENTER M15

东方商厦

In Xujiahui Commercial Area, it is a place offering visitors the convenience of shopping and spending their leisure time. It deals in retail and wholesale in food stuff, articles of daily use, suitcases and bags, cosmetics, jewelry, arts and crafts and souvenirs and household electric appliances. One-third of the commodities are imported goods. Others are products from joint-venture factories and famous brands and specialty products in the country.

PACIFIC DEPARTMENT STORE M15

太平洋百货

It is a large department store in Xujiahui Commercial Area, next to Shanghai No.6 Department Store. It caters to the general public with a great variety of commodities meeting the needs of different consumers and complete with the functions of international department stores. It offers lively, nimble and attentive "service with a smile". It pays attention to the effect of the display on the business floors, in the layout of the different floors, lighting, music, colors and arrangement of commodities, integrating aesthetics with the design of department stores.

HUIJIN DEPARTMENT STORE M15

汇金百货

◆ The department store collects a large quantity of present-day fashionable goods, among which are many internationally renown brands, meeting the needs of ladies as well as white-collar gentlemen.

NO.6 SHANGHAI GENERAL STORE M15

第六百货

◆ With more than 40 years of business experience, the store has a business floor of 6,015 sq.m., beautifully and elegantly arranged. It deals in household electric appliances, garments, ornaments, bedding, stationery, photographic equipment, clocks, watches and spectacles in 30,000 kinds, with excellent quality but reasonable prices. It is known as "a store for the general public", a favorite place catering to shoppers.

XUJIAHUI GREEN BELT M11

徐家汇绿地

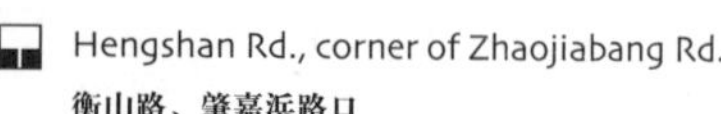

Hengshan Rd., corner of Zhaojiabang Rd.

衡山路、肇嘉浜路口

Metro line No.1, Public buses 438, 18 and 44

◆ In the northeast corner there is a lawn. Under tall trees there are 13 antique millstones collected from folk families in North China. These ancient stone pieces, though looking insignificant, can serve as seats for visitors and for their appreciation. They remind people of the old days and past folk lives.

Along some of the landscaped alleyways one can see groups of renovated "shikumen" residential quarters, which still keep the tradition of the last century but are decorated with modern facilities. The landscape around these buildings provids residents with a pleasant living environment, bringing them through the vicissitudes of history to the present modern life.

This open green belt blends urban layout, history and culture. It is dotted with modern sculptures, luxuriant trees of different species, attracting people with a far-sight into future prosperity.

METRO CITY M15

美 罗 城

◆ Opened in 1988, it is a favorite place for Shanghai citizens to spend their leisure time in shopping, catering and amusement.

* Bainaohui Information Square—Being the leader of IT retail in China, it offers services in retail business of supply, repair and play of computers. This is a place convenient for consumers to appreciate the secrets of the computer world and purchase what they need and enjoy good services after purchase.

* Street of Spectacles—It collects a number of specialty shops offering a great variety of glasses, like the American, the Modern Optician, Hongxing Spectacles, Yashi 1000, Jingcai Glasses, etc for customers to choose.

* World of Communication—On the square there are exclusive shops selling famous brands of mobile phones from different countries, such as Motorola, ready for customers to choose.

* Storm SOS Decotheque—it is the largest bar-type descotheque in Shanghai. It can accommodate 1,000 people at one time. The ball is equipped with the world's first-class lighting, acoustic and smoke facilities. Many large entertainment activities have been held here. It is a favorite place for fashionable young people and star fans in Shanghai to spend their leisure time here.

SICHUAN ROAD (N), CHINA'S FAMOUS BRAND STREET H17

四川北路商业街

◆ Next to Nanjing Road and Huaihai Road, it is the third largest commercial street in Shanghai. The road was among the first ones built after Shanghai's opening as a treaty port. North to Suzhou Creek, the 3.7-km-long street runs from south to north in Hongkou District.

- 10:00
- 22:00
- Light Rail (Hongkou Football Stadium Station) Public buses 13, 17, 21, 19, 70 and 18

✻ Landmark architectures—New buildings like Shanghai No.7 Department Store, Duolun, Kailun and Shanghai Spring Commercial Buildings on Sichuan Road offer all kinds of high-grade and medium-grade commodities at reasonable prices. The individuality of the commercial street is "to service the wage-earning class". It has become a shopping paradise for commoners and receives an average of 900,000 customers each day.

✻ Different from Nanjing Road and Huaihai Road which are crowded with super fine quality and famous brand shops, Sichuan Road (N), aiming at "serving the wage-earning class and the common people", deals mainly in fine quality China-made goods in support of the national industries. It has become a shopping center with the most brands, best quality and most kinds. The slogan in the street, "Visit and walk other streets but buy on Sichuan Road" attracts large numbers of local citizens and visitors.

✻ In the 1990s, Sichuan Road (N) was remolded on a large scale, forming today's modernized shopping street for the general public, known as the "Shopping Street for the Common People". The shops offer a great variety of commodities of high quailty and medium-grade price. With modern electronic services, mordern tourism and cultural facilities built with surrounding landscapes and a number of famous commercial and trade enterprises, it attracts more and more local citizens and tourists from home and abroad.

DUOLUN ROAD A STREET OF CULTURAL CELEBRITIES H17

多伦路文化名人街

It is a 500-m-long street in Hongkou District and its surrounding area is an epitome of Shanghai's historical and cultural course. "A Duolun Road tells the story of a 100-year Shanghai". The great Chinese writer Lu Xun conducted most of his cultural activities here, thus forming the history of Duolun Road as "an important center of modern literature". Here, we will find museums, art galleries, exhibition halls, antiques, calligraphy and painting stores. Visitors seek reminiscences about the past while enjoying the cultural relics and sightseeing in the street.

 9:00

 17:30

021-56960588

Duolun Rd., Hongkou District
虹口区多伦路

Light Rail (Hongkou Football Stadium)
Public buses 18, 21, 231 and 939

* Exhibition Hall of Chopsticks: Collector and writer Lan Xiang founded in 1988 the first folk exhibition hall of chopsticks in Shanghai, collecting over 1,600 pairs of ancient and modern chopsticks of 980 kinds from China and overseas.

* Old Film Cafe entertains you with coffee and old films of the 1920s and 1930s and displays old newspapers like "Shen Bao" and "Liangyou Film Magazine" and writings of famous stars, telling you the stories of the city of the past.

* Museum of Coins displays over 10,000 pieces of coins of 8,000 kinds, dating from the Former Qin Dynasty (475-221 B.C.) to the Nationalist regime, including precious pieces of different historical periods and those now circulating in 187 countries and regions in the world.

* Strange Stone Museum has collected more than 10,000 pieces of strange and curio stones of 100 stone material in 8 big categories: modeled stones, veined stones, biological fossils, mineral crystals, stationery blocks, memorial tablets, jade stones and handicrafts.

* Exhibition Hall of Badges of Mao Zedong: Mr. Huang Miaoxin has spent several dozens of years to collect over 28,000 badges of 33 kinds of material, like gold, silver, bamboo and jade. Here on display are only one-third of his collection.

SUPERBRAND MALL J18

正大广场

◆ Located in the center of Pudong New Area, the mall, together with the Oriental Pearl TV Tower and Jinmao Tower, is the pride of Shanghai people and the prospects of their future.

The mall was designed by an internationally well-known designing firm and is considered the largest shopping center in China. A friendly and warm atmosphere attracts shoppers with the most up-to-date fashion.

There are world-class brands from Hong Kong, French, Thai and Taiwan that cater to the favor of young people. In "Moda Thai" you can find first-rate fine quality products from Thailand.

In the mall you can experience the transformation in China from the traditional to Soho fashion.

On the 2nd to 4th floors, there are respectively fashions of the East and the West. On the 6th floor there is a mixture of the Eastern and Western fashions. In the mall you will be brought to a Suzhou Old Street, where you may experience the traditional Chinese life-style and architectural style. Then you may visit the Soho Area of China in the new century.

There you may also enjoy a show of China's tops and reminiscence of Shanghai's 100-year history. There is also an exhibition of world's tops, like the biggest pizza in China.

Superbrand Mall is a one-stop shop, in which you may enjoy all the pleasure of shopping. While you do shop

QIPU ROAD GARMENTS MARKET

七浦路服装市场

Qipu Rd., corner of Henan Rd.

河南北路、七浦路口

♦ A large garment market with an investment of 1 billion yuan and covering an area of over 10,000 sq.m., it starts booming recently. Thousands of businessmen come here to find opportunities. Products here are also sold to different parts of the country. It has become a center for collection and distribution of garments for Shanghai and its surrounding areas.

The market is classified into men's clothes, women's clothes, children's clothes, clothes for the middle-aged and the seniors and further into different textiles to meet special needs of consumer groups.

It has become a pluralistic garment consumer market, where picky customers may find what they hope to get. The facilities here are up to 5A-grade standard.

---

ping in Lotus Super Center, your children may have a good time in the children's playground. Superbrand Mall is a happy land for all.

It has genuine Thai food, besides all kinds of Western and Eastern delicacies for your choice.

No. 168 Lujiazui Rd. (W)

陆家嘴西路 168 号

Metro line No.2 (Lujiazui Station)

SPECIAL PRODUCTS OF SHANGHAI

上海特产、名店、名品

Wang Jia Sha Restaurant 王家沙点心

Its specialties are crispy meat cakes, crispy cakes with red puree filling, chicken meat stir-fried dumplings and fried noodles.

021-62586373

No. 805 Nanjing Rd. (W) 南京西路805号

Public buses 20, 37 and 23

Shen Da Cheng Restaurant 沈大成点心

It is a well-known 100-year-old restaurant, mainly serving glutinous rice dumplings, specially "yuanxiao", green dumpling, "zongzi", "wonton" with shrimps and "shaomai" with shrimps.

021-63225615

No. 636 Nanjing Rd. (E) 南京东路 636 号

Metro line No.2 (People Square Station) Public buses 20 and 37

Xian De Lai Restaurant

鲜得来排骨年糕

Yunnan Rd. street of Delicacies

云南南路美食街

Qiao Jia Zha Restaurant 乔家栅点心

With a history of 80 years, it specializes in glutinous rice dumpling, eight-jewel rice, "zongzi", steamed puffed cake and cat's ear snack.

021-64374174

No. 336 Zhonghua Rd. 中华路 336 号

Public buses 42, 119 and 926

You Lian fried meat dumpling

友联生煎

All over the city 全市分布

Shen Yu fried meat dumpling

丰裕生煎（连锁店）

All over the city 全市分布

Nan Xiang meat with steamed buns

南翔小笼

Yunnan Rd. street of Delicacies, Yuyuan Garden Commercial City 云南南路美食街豫园商城内

Lv Bo Lang Restaurant 绿波廊宁波汤团

Its specialties are steamed crab meat dumpling, steamed "jiaozi" with vegetable and meat filling, crispy cake with date puree and eye-brow-shaped crispy cake with fillings of three kinds of delicacies.

021-63737020

No. 131 Yuyuan Rd. 豫园路 131 号

Public buses 11, 65 and 126.

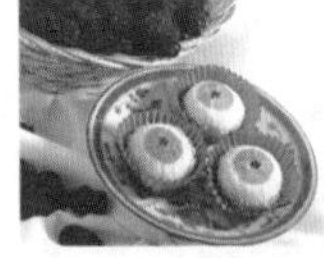

Xing Hua Lou Restaurant 杏花楼

Its specialties are creamy sliced fish, beef in oyster sauce and stewed chicken and snake. The restaurant is also famous for its Cantonese-style moon cakes.

021-63553777
No. 343 Fuzhou Rd. 福州路343号
Public buses 17, 49, 123 and 66

Sunya Cantonese Restaurant 新雅粤菜馆

Its dishes are noted for their light, smooth, fresh, tender and palatable flavor, specialized in original taste. Its specialties are stir-fried shelled shrimps and steamed winter melon soup and Cantonese snacks.

021-63517788
No. 719 Nanjing Rd. (E) 南京东路719号
Metro line No.2 (People Square Station) Public buses 18,20, 37 and 902

Meilongzhen Restaurant 梅龙镇酒店

Its specialties are Meilongzhen chicken, bean-curd cooked with longan and sliced partridge cooked with celery.

021-62566705
Lane 1081, No. 22 Nanjing Rd. (W) 南京西路1081弄22号
Metro line No.2 (Shimen Rd. 1 Rd. Station) Public buses20, 23 and 112

Sanyang Store of Delicacies from South China 三阳南货

No. 634 Nanjing Rd. (E), corner of Zhejiang Rd. (M) 南京东路、浙江中路口

Shaowansheng Store of Delicacies from South China 邵万生南货

021-63223907
No. 414 Nanjing Rd. (E) 南京东路414号
Public buses 20, 37 and 921

Zhangxiaoquan Scissors Store 张小泉剪刀

021-63223858
No. 490 Nanjing Rd. (E) 南京东路490号
Metro line No.2 (Henan Rd. Station) Public buses 20, 37 and 921

Shanghai Maochang Spectacles Store 上海茂昌眼睛公司

It's an old store with a history of a hundred years. It has made great efforts in adopting new hi-tech in developing its business. Its monthly sales volume reaches on the average of 5.8 million yuan, ranking the first in the country. By adopting advanced optometry and glasses prescription and with the skill of its technical staff, it has formed a chain business on a large scale with top quality.

9:00-21:00
021-63223839
No. 762 Nanjing Rd. (E) (in Pedestrian Walkwy) 南京东路762号（步行街内）
Metro line No.2 (Henan Rd Station), Public buses 20, 37 and 921

Jinshan Farmers' Painting Studio 金山农民画

The Exhibition of Jinshan Farmers' Paintings has been touring to the United States, Germany, France, Japan, Canada, Australia, Norway, Switzerland, Hong Kong and Taiwan. They have been greatly appreciated by visitors there. Some of the museums and art collectors in these countries and regions have collected the paintings. In January 1998, the Jinshan Farmers' Painting Studio was set up.

021-57321363
Zhujing Town, Jinshan District 金山区朱泾镇

Star	Name	Add	Tel(021)	Room Rate(RMB)
★★★★★	FOUR SEASONS HOTEL SHANGHAI	No. 500 Weihai Rd.	62568888	375-6046 (USD)
★★★★★	GRAND HYATT SHANGHAI	No. 88 Century Boulevard, Pudong	50471234	2950-42000
★★★★★	HILTON SHANGHAI	No. 250 Huashan Rd.	62480000	244-2200 (USD)
★★★★★	HONG QIAO STATE GUEST HOTEL	No. 1591 Hongqiao Rd.	62198855	200-10000 (USD)
★★★★★	HUA TING HOTEL & TOWERS	No. 1200 Caoxi Rd. (N)	64396000	215-1800 (USD)
★★★★★	INTERCONTINENTAL PUDONG SHANGHAI	No. 777 Zhangyang Rd., Pudong	58356666	2366-25666
★★★★★	JIN JIANG HOTEL	No. 59 Maoming Rd. (S)	62582582	195-3000 (USD)
★★★★★	JIN JIANG TOWER	No. 161Changle Rd.	64151188	190-3000 (USD)
★★★★★	JW MARRIOTT HOTEL SHNGHI	No. 399 Nanjing Rd. (E)	53594969	
★★★★★	OKURA GARDEN HOTEL SHANGHAI	No. 58 Maoming Rd. (S)	64151111	250-3000 (USD)
★★★★★	PEACE HOTEL	No. 20 Nanjing Rd. (E)	63216888	120-520 (USD)
★★★★★	PUDONG SHANGRI-LA	No. 33 Fucheng Rd., Pudong	68828888	320-3900 (USD)
★★★★★	PURPLE MOUNTAIN HOTEL	No. 778 Dongfang Rd., Pudong	68868888	220-3000 (USD)
★★★★★	RADISSON PLAZA XING GUO HOTEL SHANGHAI	No. 78 Xingguo Rd.	62129998	1830-41500
★★★★★	REGAL INTERNATIONAL EAST ASIA HOTEL	No. 516 Hengshan Rd.	64155588	2490-45650
★★★★★	RENAISSANCE YANGTZE SHANGHAI HOTEL	No. 2099 Yan'an Rd. (W)	62750000	250-1800 (USD)
★★★★★	SHANGHAI INTERNATIONAL CONVENTION CENTRE ORIENTAL RIVERSIDE HOTEL	No. 2727 Riverside Promenade, Pudong	50370000	280-3000 (USD)
★★★★★	SHANGHAI JC MANDARIN	No. 1225 Nanjing Rd. (W)	62791888	1945-10735
★★★★★	SHANGHAI MARRIOTT HOTEL HONGQIAO	No. 2270 Hongqiao Rd.	62376000	230-2500 (USD)
★★★★★	SHERATON GRAND TAI PING YANG SHANGHAI	No. 5 Zunyi Rd. (S)	62758888	250-2888 (USD)
★★★★★	SOFITEL JIN JIANG ORIENTAL PUDONG SHANGHAI	No. 889 Yanggao Rd. (S)	50504888	260-3000 (USD)
★★★★★	THE PORTMAN RITZ-CARLTON SHANGHAI	No. 1376 Nanjing Rd. (W)	62798888	350-4800 (USD)
★★★★★	THE ST. REGIS SHANGHAI	No. 889 Dongfang Rd.	50504567	320-4500 (USD)
★★★★★	THE WESTIN SHANGHAI	No. 88 Henan Rd. (M)	63351888	2988-31540
★★★★★	XIJIAO STATE GUEST HOTEL	No. 1921 Hongqiao Rd.	62198800	1494-5810
★★★★	BAO AN HOTEL	No. 800 Dongfang Rd.	51159888	120-600 (USD)
★★★★	BAO STEEL GROUP BAO SHAN HOTEL	No. 1813 Mudanjiang Rd.	56698888	600-8800
★★★★	BAOLONG HOTEL	No. 180 Yixian Rd.	65425425	950-8500
★★★★	BROADWAY MASIONS HOTEL	No. 20 Suzhou Rd. (N)	63246260	115-960 (USD)
★★★★	CENTRAL HOTEL SHANGHAI	No. 555 Jiujiang Rd.	53965000	180-1500 (USD)
★★★★	CITY HOTEL SHANGHAI	No. 5-7 Shaanxi Rd. (S)	62551133	1300-3000
★★★★	COURTYARD BY MARRIOTT SHANGHAI-PUDONG	No. 838 Dongfang Rd.	68867886	260-1800 (USD)
★★★★	CROWNE PLAZA SHANGHAI	No. 400 Fanyu Rd.	62808888	210-800 (USD)
★★★★	DONGHU HOTEL	No. 70 Donghu Rd.	64158158	
★★★★	GALAXY HOTEL	No. 888 Zhongshan Rd. (W)	62755888	160-1000 (USD)
★★★★	GOLDEN JADE SUNSHINE HOTEL	No. 1888 Zhoujiazui Rd.	61001888	1145-7666
★★★★	GRAND YOU YOU HOTEL SHANGHAI	No. 2111 Pudong Rd. (S)	58810888	170-1803 (USD)
★★★★	HENGSHAN HOTEL	No. 534 Hengshan Rd.	64377050	120-550 (USD)
★★★★	HOLIDAY INN DOWNTOWN SHANGHAI	No. 585 Hengfeng Rd.	63538008	140-360 (USD)
★★★★	HOLIDAY INN PUDONG SHANGHAI	No. 899 Dongfang Rd.	58306666	1500-10000
★★★★	HOLIDAY INN VISTA SHANGHAI	No. 700 Changshou Rd.	62768888	
★★★★	HOTEL EQUATORIAL SHANGHAI	No. 65 Yan'an Rd. (W)	62481688	220-1100 (USD)
★★★★	HOTEL YIHE LONGBAI SHANGHAI	No. 2451 Hongqiao Rd.	62689111	160-270 (USD)
★★★★	HOTEL ZHONGYOU INTERNATIONAL SHANGHAI	No. 969 Dongfang Rd.	68758888	1428-15120
★★★★	JIANGUO HOTEL SHANGHAI	No. 439 Caoxi Rd. (N)	64399299	96-675 (USD)
★★★★	SHANG HOTEL	No. 370 Huashan Rd.	62480088	138-628 (USD)
★★★★	NEW CENTURY HOTEL	No. 257 Siping Rd.	36084999	102-361 (USD)
★★★★	NOVOTEL ATLANTIS SHANGHAI	No. 728 Pudong Avenue	50366666	1300-16000
★★★★	OCEAN HOTEL SHANGHAI	No. 1171 Dongdaming Rd.	65458888	110-280 (USD)
★★★★	PARK HOTEL	No. 170 Nanjing Rd. (W)	63275225	80-600 (USD)
★★★★	RADISSON SAS LANSHENG HOTEL SHANGHAI	No. 1000 Quyang Rd.	55888000	160-1000 (USD)
★★★★	RAINBOW HOTEL	No. 2000 Yan'an Rd. (W)	62753388	160-470 (USD)
★★★★	RAMADA PLAZA PUDONG SHANGHAI	No. 18 Xinjinqiao Rd., Pudong	50554666	1180-3600
★★★★	RAMADA PUDONG AIRPORT SHANGHAI	No. 1100 Qihang Rd., Pudong Airport	38494949	100-1200 (USD)
★★★★	RAMADA PLAZA SHANGHAI	No. 719 Nanjing Rd. (E)	63500000	150-880 (USD)
★★★★	RENDEZVOUS MERRY HOTEL SHANGHAI	No. 396 Yan'an Rd. (W)	62495588	180-800 (USD)
★★★★	REGAL SHANGHAI EAST ASIA HOTEL	No. 800 Lingling Rd.	64266888	1280-2080
★★★★	ROYALTON HOTEL	No. 789 Wuyi Rd.	52068000	150-800 (USD)
★★★★	SEAGULL HOTEL	No. 60 Huangpu Rd.	63251500	99-650 (USD)
★★★★	SHANGHAI EVERBRIGHT CONVENTION EXHIBITION CENTER INTERNATIONAL HOTEL	No. 66 Caobao Rd.	64842500	1280-4980
★★★★	SHANGHAI WORLDFIELD CONVENTION HOTEL	No. 2106 Hongqiao Rd.	62703388	170-1000 (USD)
★★★★	SOFITEL HYLAND SHANGHAI	No. 505 Nanjing Rd. (E)	63515888	185-1200 (USD)
★★★★	THE BUND HOTEL	No. 525 Guangdong Rd.	63522000	
★★★★	TONG MAO HOTEL	No. 357 Songlin Rd., Pudong	58300000	140-460(USD)
★★★★	YING YUAN HOTEL	No. 150 Qinghe Rd., Jiading	59520952	
★★★★	YUEHUA HOTEL	No. 88 Jianghai Rd., Fengxian	57181888	700-4880
★★★	ASTRONAUTICS HOTEL	No. 222 Caoxi Rd.	64708188	380-1200
★★★	ASTOR HOUSE HOTEL	No. 15 Huangpu Rd.	63246388	420-2800
★★★	BAILEMEN HOTEL	No. 1728 Nanjing Rd. (W)	62488686	363-1320
★★★	BOTHLAND HOTEL	No. 270 Yixian Rd.	65428800	380-988
★★★	CHANGHANG MERRYLIN HOTEL	No. 818 Zhangyang Rd., Pudong	58355555	550-1680
★★★	DAZHONG HOTEL	No. 1515 Zhongshan Rd. (W)	64288888	580-1280
★★★	DIANSHAN LAKE FOREST HOLIDAY	No. 8185 Huqingping Highway	59291266	328-2380
★★★	EAST CHINA HOTEL SHAGNHAI	No. 111Tianmu Rd. (W)	63178000	780-2340
★★★	FAR EAST HOTEL	No. 600 Hengfeng Rd.	63178900	480-1580
★★★	FOREST HOTEL	No. Sheshan Pagoda	57651160	350-
★★★	GAN YUAN HOTEL	No. 417 Yuyao Rd.	62727258	360-1008
★★★	GAO QIAO PETRO-CHENICAL HOTEL	No. 2998 Pudong Avenue	58712633	350-1280
★★★	HAI YAN HOTEL	No. 325 Baoding Rd.	65122060	388-800
★★★	HENGSHAN COMFOTEL	No. 88 Chengnan Rd., Huinan Town, Nanhui	58000000	330-1880

LIST OF MAIN HOTELS 主要宾馆、酒店一览

Star	Name	Add	Tel(021)	Room Rate(RMB)
★★★	HONGGANG HOTEL	No. 2550 Hongqiao Rd.	62681008	300-2800
★★★	HONGLOU HOTEL	No. 1 Puzhao Rd., Songjiang	57822812	60-120 (USD)
★★★	HONG HOTEL	No. 158 Changchun Rd.	56718800	62-106 (USD)
★★★	HOTEL YUANLIN SHANGHAI	No. 100 Baise Rd.	54361688	80-300 (USD)
★★★	HUAJING GRAND HOTEL	No. 1687 Changyang Rd.	65189988	
★★★	HUA MAO HOTEL	No. 2550 Hongqiao Rd.	62682266	400-1000
★★★	HUA TING GUEST HOUSE	No. 2525 Zhongshan Rd. (W)	64813500	680-1500
★★★	HOMEYO HOTEL	No. 2550 Hongqiao Rd.	62689999	385-1650
★★★	HUAXIA HOTEL	No. 38 Caobao Rd.	64360100	40-120 (USD)
★★★	HUAYING YUANBO HOTEL	No. 1188 Changshou Rd.	62526858	498-1800
★★★	HUI YUAN HOTEL	No. 398 Chengnan Rd., Huinan Town	58020000	300-2800
★★★	HUNAN HOTEL	No. 1243 Zhongshan Rd. (W)	62752468	498-1528
★★★	JIADING HOTEL	No. 100 Bole Rd., Jiading	59525512	380-9999
★★★	JIADING MEETING CENTRE OF SHANGHAI CUSTOMS	No. 257 Jialuo Rd., Jiading	59166258	480-2500
★★★	JIANGSU HOTEL	No. 888 Wuning Rd.	62051888	60-158 (USD)
★★★	JIANG TIAN HOTEL	No. 3456 Pudong Rd. (S)	58705870	300-1800
★★★	JIN CHANG HOTEL SHANGHAI	No. 1339 Changde Rd.	62988899	
★★★	JINCHEN HOTEL	No. 795-809 Huaihai Rd. (M)	64717000	680-1180
★★★	JIN FU MEN HOTEL	No. 1285 Mudanjiang Rd.	56116666	480-1200
★★★	JIN LI HUA HOTEL	No. 5007 Chuansha Rd., Pudong	58923700	480-1688
★★★	JIN QIAO HOTEL	No. 1379 Jinqiao Rd., Pudong	58990890	92-160 (USD)
★★★	JIN SHA HOTEL	No. 257 Nujiang Rd.	62578888	52-203 (USD)
★★★	JIN XUAN HOTEL	No. 238 Nandan Rd. (E)	64682222	250-888
★★★	JIULONG HOTEL	No. 601 Liyang Rd.	65418228	440-1980
★★★	JU YUAN HOLIDAY RESORT	No. Changxing Island, Baoshan District	66852508	280-580
★★★	LAN SUN MOUNTAIN VILLA	No. Moutain feet of Sheshan	57651170	
★★★	LIU DAO HOLIDAYS VILLAGE SHANGHAI	No. Liu Island, Jiading	59950464	
★★★	LONG HUA HOTEL	No. 2787 Longhua Rd.	64570570	368-1688
★★★	LONGMEN HOTEL	No. 777 Hengfeng Rd.	63170000	60-230 (USD)
★★★	LU YUAN HOTEL	No. 39 Waixiangua Rd.	63306060	300-1800
★★★	MAGNOLIA HOTEL	No. 1251 Siping Rd.	65026888	45-200 (USD)
★★★	MASON HOTEL SHANGHAI	No. 935 Huaihai Rd. (M)	64662020	
★★★	MEI LI HUA HOLIDAY VILLA	No. 5000 Cao'an Rd.	59592588	418-2178
★★★	METROPOLE HOTEL	No. 180 Jiangxi Rd. (M)	63213030	550-1200
★★★	NANHUAYUAN HOLIDAY RESORT	No. 969 Huateng Rd., Qingpu	59794100	480-2000
★★★	NEW ASIA HOTEL	No. 422 Tiantong Rd.	63242210	47-360 (USD)
★★★	NEW GARDEN HOTEL	No. 1900 Hongqiao Rd.	62426688	60-300 (USD)
★★★	OASIS TOWER	No. 555 Zhongshan Rd. (W)	62865888	480-680
★★★	PACIFIC LUCK HOTEL	No. 299 Wusong Rd.	63259800	82-145 (USD)
★★★	PINE CITY HOTEL	No. 777 Zaojiabang Rd.	64433888	650-3000
★★★	PUDONG HOTEL	No. 1888 Pudong Rd. (S)	68758800	480-980
★★★	QIANHE HOTEL	No. 650 Yishan Rd.	64700000	500-3200
★★★	QIGNPU HOTEL	No. 79 Chengzhong Rd. (N), Qingpu	59850688	320-880
★★★	QING ZHI LU HOTEL	No. 219 Wending Rd.	64690808	628-1280
★★★	RIVERSIDE HOTEL SHANGHAI	No. 1305 Kaixuan Rd. (N)	62609988	658-1288
★★★	RAMADA SHANGHAI CAOHEJING HOTEL	No. 509 Caobao Rd.	54649999	480-1280
★★★	RENHE HOTEL	No. 2056 Pudong Avenue	58601688	380-980
★★★	SENTOSA HOTEL	No. 1 Nanqiao Rd., Fengxian	57429999	598-4980
★★★	SHANGHAI AUTOMOBILE INDUSTRY ACTIVITIES CENTRE BLUE PALACE HOTEL	No. 125 Bole Rd. (S), Jiading	59161000	420-6000
★★★	SHANGHAI BAO DAO RESORT	South of Dongping State Forest Park	59339898	466-8800
★★★	SHANGHAI DAQING OIL MANSION	No. 1515 Zhongshan Rd. (E2)	65559191	480-4000
★★★	SHANGHAI JINMING HOTEL	No. 2088 Caoyang Rd.	52781888	580-4880
★★★	JIN SHAN HOTEL	No. 1 Jinyi Rd. (E), Jinshan District	57941888	240-2500
★★★	SHANGHAI CCECC PLAZA HOTEL	No. 666 New Gonghe Rd.	56721188	580-2460
★★★	SHANGHAI CLASSICAL HOTEL	No. 242 Fuyou Rd.	63111777	428-1278
★★★	SHANGHAI CONVENTION CENTER, CHINESE ACADEMY OF SCIENCES ANOTHER NAME: HOPE HOTEL	No. 500 Zaojiabang Rd.	64716060	50-375 (USD)
★★★	SHANGHAI DECON ENTERTAINMENT CITY	No. 555 Gongkang Rd.	56408555	450-2580
★★★	SHANGHAI FAN YANG DOWNTOWN RESORT	No. 55 Yuyao Rd.	32204567	680-2800
★★★	SHANGHAI GANGHONG HOTEL	No. 501 Wuning Rd.	62868800	528-3800
★★★	SHANGHAI GOLDEN SEASIDE RESORT	Sea Holiday Resort, Nanhui	58058858	288-1980
★★★	SHANGHAI GUHUA GARDEN HOTEL	No. 276 Jiefang Rd. (M), Fengxian	67181300	480-8880
★★★	SHANGHAI HANSEN HOTEL	No. 302 Fanyu Rd.	62830355	360-850
★★★	SHANGHAI HOPE GARDEN HOTEL	No. 2599 Huyi Highway, Malu Town	59158989	380-1580
★★★	SHANGHAI HUIHENG NEW ASIA HOTEL	No. 168 Tongji Rd., Huinan Town, Nanhui	58010000	400-1800
★★★	SHANGHAI INTERNATIONAL AIRPORT HOTEL	No. 2550 Hongqiao Rd.	62688866	650-1860
★★★	SHANGHAI INTERNATIONAL BOWLING RESORT	No. 2938 Jindu Rd.	64582000	480-1680
★★★	SHANGHAI JIANGONG JINJIANG HOTEL	No. 691 Jianguo Rd. (W)	64155688	752-1987
★★★	SHANGHAI JINHUI HOTEL	No. 8 Wuzhong Rd.	64282222	550-1680
★★★	SHANGHAI JINJIANG DAHUA HOTEL	No. 918 Yan'an Rd. (W)	62512512	70-130 (USD)
★★★	SHANGHAI JINYAN HOTEL	No. 3800 Chunshen Rd.	54150000	480-1200
★★★	SHANGHAI KUNMINGHU HOTEL VILLAGE	No. 18 Hongyun Rd.,Fengxian	57130500	400-4000
★★★	SHANGHAI LIANGAN HOTEL	No. 920 Chang'an Rd.	63532222	298-2280
★★★	SHANGHAI MINGREN YUAN GARDEN HOTEL	No. 2988 Zhangyang Rd.	58852988	380-980
★★★	SHANGHAI PEARL HOTEL	No. 212 Zaojiabang Rd.	64310880	229-2288
★★★	SHANGHAI OLYMPIC HOTEL	No. 1800 Zhongshan Rd. (S2)	64391391	650-2800
★★★	SHANGHAI ORIENTAL GREEN BOAT HOLIDAY RESORT	No. 6888 Huqingping Highway	59233388	330-780
★★★	SHANGHAI PACIFIC HOTEL (FORMER HUA QIAO HOTEL)	No. 108 Nanjing Rd. (W)	63276226	280-2500
★★★	SHANGHAI PIAOYING HOTEL	No. 71 Zhapu Rd.	63240118	
★★★	SHANGHAI POST & TELECOMMUNICATIONS HOTEL	No. 601 Hengfeng Rd.	63178888	388-2000
★★★	HANGHAI SHUANYONG HOTEL	No. 2601 Pudong Avenue	58718898	368-1688

Star	Name	Add	Tel(021)	Room Rate(RMB)
★★★	SHANGHAI SWAN HOTEL	No. 2211 Sichuan Rd. (N)	56665666	75-140 (USD)
★★★	SHANGHAI TAO-CHENG RESORT	No. 9191 Hunan Highway	58003158	
★★★	SHANGHAI WAIGAOQIAO FREE TRADE ZONG HOTEL	No. 8 Xiabi Rd.	58620000	
★★★	SHANGHAI WUMAO HOTEL	No. 2550 Zhongshan Rd. (N)	62570000	466-1880
★★★	SHANGHAI XINCI HOTEL	No. 29 Antingmoyu Rd., Jiading	59568888	400-900
★★★	SHANGHAI XINGYU HOTEL	No. 386 Renmin Rd.	63338888	180-2280
★★★	SHANGHAI ZHONGDIAN HOTEL	No. 1029 Laoshan Rd. (W), Pudong	58798798	480-1280
★★★	SHANGHAI ZHONGFU MANSION	No. 619 Jiujiang Rd.	53594900	560-1050
★★★	S.I. JAHWA TRAINING CENTRE	No. 1 Nanhuan Rd., Zhoujiajiao Town,Qingpu District	59248100	328-3880
★★★	SILK ROAD HOTEL	No. 777 Quyang Rd.	65549988	358-2888
★★★	SIMI HOTEL	No. 305 Qixin Rd.	64881888	480-1088
★★★	SOUTH COMMERCIAL CENTER HOTEL	No. 7388 Humin Rd.	64123888	380-920
★★★	SPORTS HOTEL	No. 15 Nandan Rd.	64382222	588-1580
★★★	SUNRISE HOTEL	No. 128 Hangzhou Bay Avenue Jinshan Petroleum	57282828	480-2800
★★★	SUN & MOON ISLAND HOLIDAY RESORT	No. 8700 Huqingping Highway	59262960	380-980
★★★	TIAN HE HOTEL	No. 178 Qiaonan Rd., Chongming County	69690000	380-1510
★★★	TIANLIN HOTEL	No. 1 Tianlin Rd.	64367070	60-420 (USD)
★★★	TIAN PING HOTEL	No. 185 Tianping Rd.	54514567	380-4800
★★★	TONG XIN HOTEL	No. 618 Yecheng Rd.	59166777	528-888
★★★	WEST ASIA HOTEL	No. 20 Tianyaoqiao Rd.	64872000	580-1640
★★★	WINDSOR EVERGREEN HOTEL	No. 88 Baise Rd.	54350888	80-310 (USD)
★★★	WISTARIA HOTEL	No. 3050 Dongchuan Rd.	64301888	360-980
★★★	WU GONG HOTEL	No. 431 Fuzhou Rd.	63260303	260-1280
★★★	XIAYUAN HOTEL	No. 1081 Mudanjiang Rd.	56161918	240-1888
★★★	XIE TONG HOTEL	No. 4671 Cao'an Rd.	59595858	450-1880
★★★	XIN MIN HOTEL	No. 701 Hutai Rd.	56081188	338-888
★★★	XINCHENG HOTEL	No. 199 Kaicheng Rd.	54151500	188-888
★★★	XINDONGFANG HOTEL SHANGHAI	No. 525 Zhenning Rd.	62266800	580-1180
★★★	XING HUA HOTEL	No. 1226 Huashan Rd.	62260123	680-2980
★★★	YANAN HOTEL	No. 1111 Yan'an Rd. (M)	62481111	600-3000
★★★	YANGTZE HOTEL	No. 740 Hankou Rd.	63517880	450-1480
★★★	YIN FA HOTEL	No. 1068 Beijing Rd. (W)	62556600	588-1588
★★★	Y. M. C. A. HOTEL	No. 123 Xizang Rd. (S)	63261040	48-178 (USD)
★★★	YUPING HOTEL	No. 448 Zunyi Rd.	62333448	50-320 (USD)
★★★	ZHAO AN HOTEL	No. 195 Hengtong Rd.	63172221	668-1248
★★★	ZHONGYA HOTEL	No. 330 Meiyuan Rd.	63172317	380-1000
	Part of 2 star hotels in central Shanghai			
★★	Bayi Guesthouse	No. 888 Quyang Rd.	65535288	220-580
★★	Baisha Hotel	No. 1755 Sichuan Rd. (N)	65405555	370-2680
★★	Bailemen Hotel	No. 1728 Nanjing Rd. (W)	62488686	230-600
★★	Beiren Hotel	No. 2250 Zhongshan Rd. (N)	62542100	380-990
★★	North Sea Hotel	No. 1500 Wuning Rd.	62549521	280-1800
★★	Chunshenjiang Hotel	No. 626 Nanjing Rd. (E)	63515710	260-880
★★	Metropolis Hotel	No. 131 Hubei Rd.	63226800	210-800
★★	Donghong Hotel	No. 1161 Dongdaming Rd.	65455008	230-1200
★★	East China Sea Hotel	No. 279 Pudong Avenue	58878687	420-480
★★	East Asia Hotel	No. 680 Nanjing Rd. (E)	63223223	300-600
★★	Gongxiao Hotel	No. 1 Hengfeng Rd.	63801818	120-600
★★	Harbor Hotel	No. 89 Taixing Rd.	62553553	30-75 (USD)
★★	Heibei Hotel	No. 57 Lane 749, Tianmu Rd. (M)	63531066	30-100
★★	Huatian Holiday Hotel	No. 469 Zhonghuaxin Rd.	56300088	288-900
★★	Lufang Building	No. 670 Shaanxi Rd. (N)	62551249	300-800
★★	Huijinglou Hotel	No. 1088 Lujiabang Rd.	63762282	220-980
★★	Shanghai International Culture Exchange Center	No. 555 Chifeng Rd.	65318882	328-1008
★★	Jiuyang Hotel	No. 447 Gubei Rd.	62735100	200-380
★★	Lejiu Hotel	No. 669 Yongxin Rd.	56976969	240-600
★★	Liangliang Hotel	No. 77 Zhongshan Rd. (S)	63743969	200-1800
★★	Lidu Hotel	No. 678 Hankou Rd.	63224555	300-600
★★	Longjiang Hotel	No. 147 Dongxin Rd.	62055960	200-880
★★	Lusheng Hotel	No. 68 Taichang Rd.	53821600	210-700
★★	Luyuan Hotel	No. 39 Waixiangua Rd.	63306060	300-1800
★★	Nanjing Hotel	No. 200 Zhongshan Rd. (W)	63222888	25-100 (USD)
★★	Nanxinyuan Hotel	No. 277 Shanyin Rd.	56961187	280-580
★★	Ningxia Hotel	No. 1018 Dingxi Rd.	62110988	220-450
★★	Haiquan Hotel	No. 346 Tianshan Rd.	62730200	178-500
★★	Seven Sky Hotel	No. 627 Nanjing Rd. (E)	63220777	280-3500
★★	Shanghai International Education Exchange Center	No. 55 Guilin Rd.	64360440	130-5000
★★	Shanghai Jiangong Guesthouse	No. 1933 Xinzha Rd.	62580557	200-520
★★	Shanghai Liangyou Hotel	No. 1455 Suzhou Rd. (S)	62873663	37-68 (USD)
★★	Shanghai Nanya Hotel	No. 1280 Zhongshan Rd. (S)	63761916	140-240
★★	Shanghai Piaoying Hotel	No. 71 Zhapu Rd.	63240118	88-39 (USD)
★★	Railway Hotel	No. 160 Guizhou Rd.	63226633	280-1980
★★	Tianyi Hotel	No. 1805 Siping Rd.	65650155	200-2180
★★	Ting Feng Hotel	No. 1031 Dingxi Rd.	62100003	198-880
★★	Xianxia Hotel	No. 555 Shuicheng Rd.	62419600	350-600
★★	New Longhua Hotel	No. 288 Liuzhou Rd. (S)	64956404	260-880
★★	Yuanjing Hotel	No. 1049 Hutai Rd.	56619023	280-1400
★★	Jinjiangzhixing Chain Hotel	9th floor of Lianyi Building, No.100 Yan'an Rd. (E)	64514556	

SHANGHAI HOSPITAL 医院一览

Name	Address	Telephone
Shanghai Medical Emergency Center	No. 638 Yishan Rd.	021-24027777
Shanghai No.1 People's Hospital	No. 85 Wujin Rd.	021-63240090
Shanghai No.2 People's Hospital	No. 1 Duojia Rd.	021-63770126
Shanghai No.5 People's Hospital	No. 801 Heqing Rd.	021-64308151
Shanghai No.6 People's Hospital	No. 600 Yishan Rd.	021-64369181
Shanghai No.7 People's Hospital	No. 358 Datong Rd.	021-58670561
Shanghai No.8 People's Hospital	No. 8 Caobao Rd.	021-64363101
Shanghai Oriental Hospital	No. 150 Jimo Rd.	021-38804518
Shanghai Tuberculosis Hospital	No. 507 Zhengmin Rd.	021-65115006
Shanghai People's Hospital of Putuo District	No. 1291 Jiangning Rd.	021-32274550
Shanghai Second Medicl College Affiliated No.9 People's Hospital	No. 639 Zhizaoju Rd.	021-63138341
Shanghai Second Medicl College Affiliated Xinhua Hospital	No. 1665 Kongjiang Rd.	021-65790000
Shanghai Gamma Knife Hospital	No. 518 Wuzhong Rd. (E)	021-64385336
Shanghai Railway Bureau Central Hospital Affiliated Railway Hospital	No. 301 Yanchang Rd. (M)	021-56770588
Changning District Central Hospital	No. 1111 Xianxia Rd.	021-62909911
Longhua Hospital	No. 725 Wanping Rd. (S)	021-64385700
Tongji University Affiliated Tongji Hospital	No. 389 Xincun Rd.	021-56051080
East China Hospital	No. 221 Yan'an Rd. (W)	021-62483180
Yangpu District Central Hospital	No. 450 Tengyue Rd.	021-65690520
85 Hospital	No. 1328 Huashan Rd.	021-62528805
Zhabei District Central Hospital	No. 619 New Zhonghua Rd.	021-56628584
People's Hospital of Pudong New Area	No. 490 Chuanhuan Rd. (S)	021-58981990
Huangpu District Central Hospital	No. 109 Sichuan Rd. (M)	021-63212487
Huangpu District Chinese and Western Medicine Hospitals	No. 163 Huangjia Rd.	021-63774871
Pok Oi Hospital	No. 1590 Huaihai Rd. (M)	021-64312600
Ruijin Hospital	No. 197 No 2 Ruijin Rd.	021-64370045
Jing'an District Central Hospital	No. 259 Xikang Rd.	021-62474530
Shanghai Chinese Medicine Hospital	No. 274 Zhijiang Rd. (M)	021-56639828
Shanghai Children's Hospital	24 lane, No. 1400 Beijing Rd. (W)	021-62474880
Chinese Welfare Association International Peace MCH Hospital	No. 910 Hengshan Rd.	021-64070434
Fudan University Affiliated Obstetrical and Gynaecological Hospital	No. 419 Fangxie Rd.	021-63770161
Shanghai Eye Disease Prevention Center Shanghai Eye Hospital	No. 380 Kangding Rd.	021-62717733
Fudan University Affiliated Tumor Hospital	No. 270 Dong'an Rd.	021-64175590

SHANGHAI TOURISM CENTER

上海旅游集散中心

Various kinds of joint tickets (including transport and ticket) are offered here at a favorable price. Accomodation and tour guide can also be arranged here. The tourists can buy tickets, two weeks before starting, at bus starting point and Meiya chain store, or at the center that day.

There are over 60 tour lines and over 400 buses each day, receiving more than 5,000 persons each day. The tourist destinations include scenic spots in suburb Shanghai and neighboring provinces.

There are well-preserved riverside towns like Zhouzhuang, Wuzhen, Xitang and Tongli, where you can feel the Jiangnan cultre of the Ming and Qing Dynasties. There are also tour lines to appreciate Shanghai metropolitan sights with modern gardens of natural flavor.

Xuhui Bus Station (No. 666 Tianyaoqiao Rd., Southwest Shanghai)

徐汇发车点（天钥桥路 666 号，位于上海西南向）

Daily Dispatch OF Buses

	RMB
Police Museum	12.00
Shanghai Urban Planning Exhibition Center	32.00
Wuzhen tour joint ticket	110.00
Zhouzhuang tour joint ticket	110.00
Tongli tour joint ticket	110.00
Songjiang tour joint ticket	76.00
Ningbo (one-way ticket)	78.00
Nantong (one-way ticket)	45.00
Nanjing (one-way ticket)	88.00
Wuxi (one-way ticket)	39.00
Nanjing sightseeing (one-way ticket)	148.00
Oriental Pearl TV Tower tour joint ticket (one-way ticket)	52.00
Jinmao Tower tour joint ticket (one-way ticket)	52.00
Shanghai Ocean Aquarium tour joint ticket (one-way ticket)	110.00
Dayang Sea World Children's ticket (below 1.4 m)	60.00
Grand Theater-Urban shopping tour (disabled, soldiers, students)	35.00
Grand-Theater-urban shopping tour (adult, valid on that day)	55.00
Grand View Garden tour joint ticket	70.00
Zhujiajiao tour joint ticket	70.00
Happy 1 day tour of new Shanghai	88.00
Qingqing Tourism Worldtour joint ticket	65.00
Guyi Garden tour joint ticket	31.00
Wuzhen (tour guide service in the whole journey)	128.00
Zhouzhuang (tour guide service in the whole journey)	128.00
Xitang (tour guide service in the whole journey)	110.00
Shanghai Audio Visual Paradise tour joint ticket	60.00
Dayang Sea World tour joint ticket	80.00
Sunqiao Agriculture Gardentour joint ticket	33.00
Shanghai Wildlife Zoo tour joint ticket	105.00
Dongping State Forest Park, Chongming Islandtour joint ticket	76.00
Shanghai Zoo tour joint ticket (one-way ticket)	19.00

Weekend Dispatch of Buses (Saturday & Sunday)

Shanghai Night Tour	70.00
Nanxun one day tour	100.00
Xitang tour joint ticket	90.00
Changzhou Chinese Dinasaur Park	160.00
North and South Lake tour joint ticket	110.00
Dangui Garden tour joint ticket	80.00
2 day tour of Nanxun and Wuzhen	330.00
2 day tour of west Zhejiang and Shenlongchuan	380.00
2 day tour of Shaoxing and Keyan	360.00
Shajiabang (Yushan, Shang Lake) tour joint ticket	120.00
Suzhou tour joint ticket	100.00
Wuxi Ling Hilltour joint ticket	135.00
Suzhou Garden tour joint ticket	148.00
Luzhi-Panmen tour joint ticket	120.00
1 day tour of Tongli, Zhouzhuangtour joint ticket	170.00
2 day tour of Xitang, Mo's Garden tour joint ticket	330.00
2 day tour of east Tianmu Mountain, Volcano Great Valley	380.00
2 day tour of Xikou, Tingxia Lake, joint ticket	360.00
Yangcheng Lake (Tingling Park) tour joint ticket (Starts seasonally)	88.00

The Station for Starting Off in Xuhui District

Shanghai Satadium Gate 12 Staircase 5. Metro line 1 and 3 can arrive; bus 43, 15, 89, 111, 92, 42 and 104 can arrive.
Hotline: 64265555, 64266455

The Station for Starting Off in Hongkou District

Hongkou Football Stadium Gates (East Jiangwan Road No.444). Metro line 3 can arrive; bus 70, 52,51,110,552,139,18 and 21 can arrive.
Hotline:56963248

The Station for Starting Off in Yangpu District

Yangpu Sports Centre (Longchang Road No.640). Bus 145,577,77, 28,813 and Bridge Line 5 can arrive.
Hotline:65803210

Yangpu Bus Station (No. 640 Longchang Rd., Northeast Shanghai)

杨浦发车点（隆昌路 640 号，位于上海东北向）

Hongkou Bus Station (No. 444 Jiangwan Rd. (E), North Shanghai)

虹口发车点（东江湾路 444 号，位于上海北向）

Daily Dispatch OF Buses

Happy 1 day tour of new Shanghai	88.00	Zhouzhang (tour guide service)	128.00
Wuzhen (tour guide service)	128.00	Xitang (tour guide service)	110.00

Weekend Dispatch of Buses (Saturday & Sunday)

Zhouzhuang	110.00
Tongli	110.00
Xitang	90.00
Grand View Garden	70.00
North and South Lake	110.00
Ling Hill in Wuxi	135.00
Luzhi-Panmen	120.00
Grand View Garden-Zhouzhuang	140.00
Wuzhen	110.00
Mudu	100.00
Nanxun	100.00
Zhujiajiao	70.00
Shajiabang	120.00
Suzhou Garden	148.00
Tongli-Zhouzhuang	170.00
Xikou-Tingxia Lake	345.00
Changzhou Chinese Dinorsaur Garden	160.00

● including one-way ticket and entrance ticket

▲ return ticket, entrance ticket and dinner

★ Open seasonally

If there's any change, please see the information in tourism center

Tours by Train

2 day tour of Nanjing 298.00

2 day tour of Suzhou and Hangzhou 180.00

2 day tour of Suzhou and Zhouzhuang 145.00

2 day tour of Suzhou and Nanjing 328.00

2 day tour of Suzhou and Tongli 155.00

2 day tour of Suzhou and Wuxi 160.00

2 day tour of Nanxun and Wuzhen 330.00

2 day tour of west Zhejiang and Shenlongchuan 380.00

2 day tour of West Lake and Hangzhou 368.00 (all inclusive)

2 day tour of Ling Hill and Hangzhou 368.00 (all inclusive)

1 day tour of Hangzhou 208.00 (all inclusive)

2 day tour of Qiandao Lake 398.00 (all inclusive except dinner)

1 day tour of Suzhou Garden 70.00

2 day tour of Shaoxing and Keyan 380.00

2 day tour of Hangzhou, Tonglu, Yaolin 280.00

2 day tour of Qiaodao Lake and Jiangnan Shilin 438.00

2 day tour of stone Great Wall, Vocalno and Great Valley 368.00

2 day tour of of great valley in west Zhejiang and baishuijian 330.00

2 day tour of of Xitang and Mo's Garden 330.00

2 day tour of Qiandao Lake, Hangzhou 360.00

2 day tour of of East Tianmu Mountain, Volcano and Great Valley 380.00

2 day tour of of Hangzhou, Fuchunjiang River and Baiyunyuan 360.00

3 day tour ofQiandao Lake, Xin'an River and Tonglu 538.00

2 day tour of of Hangzhou, Fuchunjiang River and Qinxixiangu 280.00

PRINCIPAL SCENIC AREAS AROUND SHANGHAI
上海周边主要景区

SUZHOU 苏州

Suzhou, together with Hangzhou, has been known since ancient time as "heaven on earth". It is a historical and cultural city famous for a great number of cultural relics and classical gardens. Suzhou gardens are characterized by their graceful and delicate workmanship. Popular scenic areas are: Huqiu (Tiger Hill) with a leaning tower, 4 famous gardens of the Lingering, Master Fisherman's Net, Lion Grove and Humble Administrator, which is one of the great classical gardens in China, Hanshan Temple, Canglang Pavilion, Panmen Gate and the Tianping Hill. The traditional arts and crafts in Suzhou are silk, silk embroidery and jade carving.

HANGZHOU 杭州

Hangzhou, Zhejiang Province, is listed by the State Council as a key scenic, tourist city of long history and culture. Covering an area of 6,596 sq.m., it is one of the 7 ancient capitals in China. The picturesque and charming West Lake scenic areas, Yue Fei Temple, Pagoda of Six Harmonies, Lingyin Temple, the Running Tiger Spring and Longjing Tea Plantation Area attract thousands of tourists all year round.

WUXI 无锡

Famed as "a pearl on Taihu Lake", it is a famous city with a history of over 3,000 years. With beautiful scenery and abundant products, it is known as "a country of fish and rice". For its numerous natural and humanistic sights, it has been popularly called "the top in the country". Famous scenic areas are: Turtle Islet, Liyuan Garden, Meiyuan Garden, Lingshan Giant Buddha and China Film and TV Production Base.

SOUTH LAKE IN JIAXING 嘉兴南湖

Together with the West Lake in Hangzhou and the East Lake in Shaoxing, it forms the "three famous lakes in Zhejiang Province". The scenery on the lake is described by the poem "drizzling rain is shading the lake with fog; looking into the distance there is a vast expanse of mist". There are a fossil of a 40,000-year old blood cypress, many stone carvings, carved stone tablets and historical relics.

ZHOUZHUANG 周庄

Zhouzhuang Town, 38 k.m. away from Suzhou but neighboring the Dianshan Lake, has a history of more than 900 years. It is known as "No.1 Riverside Town in China". Famous scenic spots are: Mansion of Shen Family, known as "No.1 Family of Wealth", Double Bridge, Chengxu Taoist Temple, Mi Hall, former residence of Ye Chuchang, Decorated Archway and ancient Quanfu Temple. It used to be the distribution center of cereal, silk, pottery, porcelain and handicraft in south China.

NANXUN 南浔

Nanxunn has enjoyed the fame as "origin of Hu silk, hometown of fish and rice, town of culture and garden scener". The typical waterside village view, profound culutre tradition and unique classic garden and blended architecture make it a spotlight. In 1991, it is listed as the top town of culture and history in Zhejiang Province. It boasts silks and books and tens of thousands ancient books that are collected here. Beautiful Littel Lotus Village deserves the name of "coverpage" of Nanxun.

WUZHEN 乌镇

Wuzhen is the hometown of Mao Dun, a famous Chinese man-of-letter. His former residence is a 4-storied wood-and-brick, old-fashioned house, which is now made into an exhibition hall, displaying his photos, works, manuscripts, books and articles of daily use, describing the literary life of this great writer. It is now kept as a key cultural relic under state protection.

TONGLI 同里

The riverside town Tongli is on the Grand Canal, 20 k.m. away from Suzhou and 90 k.m. away from Shanghai. It is a typical ancient riverside town with a history of over 1,000 years. The town has a strong cultural atmosphere and many scholarly celebrities have originated from here. There are many private mansions and gardens of ancient architecture. It is known as a "Museum of Ancient Architecture". The well-known Garden of Retreat is famous for its two carved halls and three bridges.

XITANG 西塘

The ancient town Xitang is crisscrossed by a number of rivers and bridges. The town has a very quiet surrounding. It is a typical well-preserved ancient riverside town. It has not only a beautiful environment but also a strong cultural atmosphere with its long history, during which many intelligent scholars were brought up. With streams flowing under little bridges, families by the river reflecting in the water and little boats rowing under the setting sun, it is really a picture full of poetic charm. During the Spring Equinox (4th solar term) and Autumnal Equinox (16th solar term), the turbulent tides rush in thundering along like earthquake; the highest tide can reach 9-m high. It's really a magnificent view!

LUZHI 甪直

Located 18 k.m. away from Suzhou, it is a famous historical and cultural city with a history of more than 2,500 years. It has been listed as a key tourist area. Covering only an area of l sq.k.m., the town is crisscrossed by many rivers, spanned by many little bridges and flanked on both sides by ancient houses of the Ming and Qing Dynasties. There are altogether 41 ancient bridges of the Song, Yuan, Ming and Qing Dynasties; the town is therefore known as a "Museum of Bridges in China". Famous scenic spots are: Baosheng Temple, Memorial Hall of Ye Shengtao, Wansheng Rice Store, Tomb of Lu Guimeng, a Tang Dynasty poet, Museum of Costumes of Riverside Town Women and Memorial Hall of Wang Tao, one of the founders of Chinese newspapers.

SEEING TIDES IN HAINING 海宁观潮

Built after liberation, the 308-k.m.-long embankment is the best place to see tides. The shape of river bed is like a special trumpet mouth shape. The widest is over 100 km, and the narrowest is 3.69 km. Thus the tide is very magnificent with a height of over 9 meters.

上海轨道交通示意图 Shanghai Rail Transit Map

共富新村
Gongfu Xincun S.
呼兰路
Hulan Rd. S.
通河新村
Tonghe Xincun S.
共康路
Gongkang Rd. S.
彭浦新村
Pengpu Xincun S.
汶水路
Wenshui Rd. S.
上海马戏城
Shanghai Circus City S.
延长路
Yanchang Rd. S.
中山北路
Zhongshan Rd.(N) S.
上海火车站
Shanghai Railway Station S.
汉中路
江湾镇
Jiangwan Town S.
汶水东路
Wenshui Rd.(E) S.
赤峰路
Chifeng Rd. S.
虹口足球场
Hongkou Football Stadium S.
东宝兴路
Baoxing Rd.(E) S.
宝山路
Baoshan Rd. S.
新闸路
Xinzha Rd. S.
河南中路
Henan Rd.(M) S.
海伦路
Hailun Rd. S.
临平路
Linping Rd. S.
陆家嘴
Lujiazui S.
东昌路
大连路
Dalian Rd. S.
杨树浦路
Yangshupu Rd. S.
浦东大道
Pudong Avenue S.
中潭路
Zhongtan Rd. S.
镇坪路
Zhenping Rd. S.
曹杨路
Caoyang Rd. S.

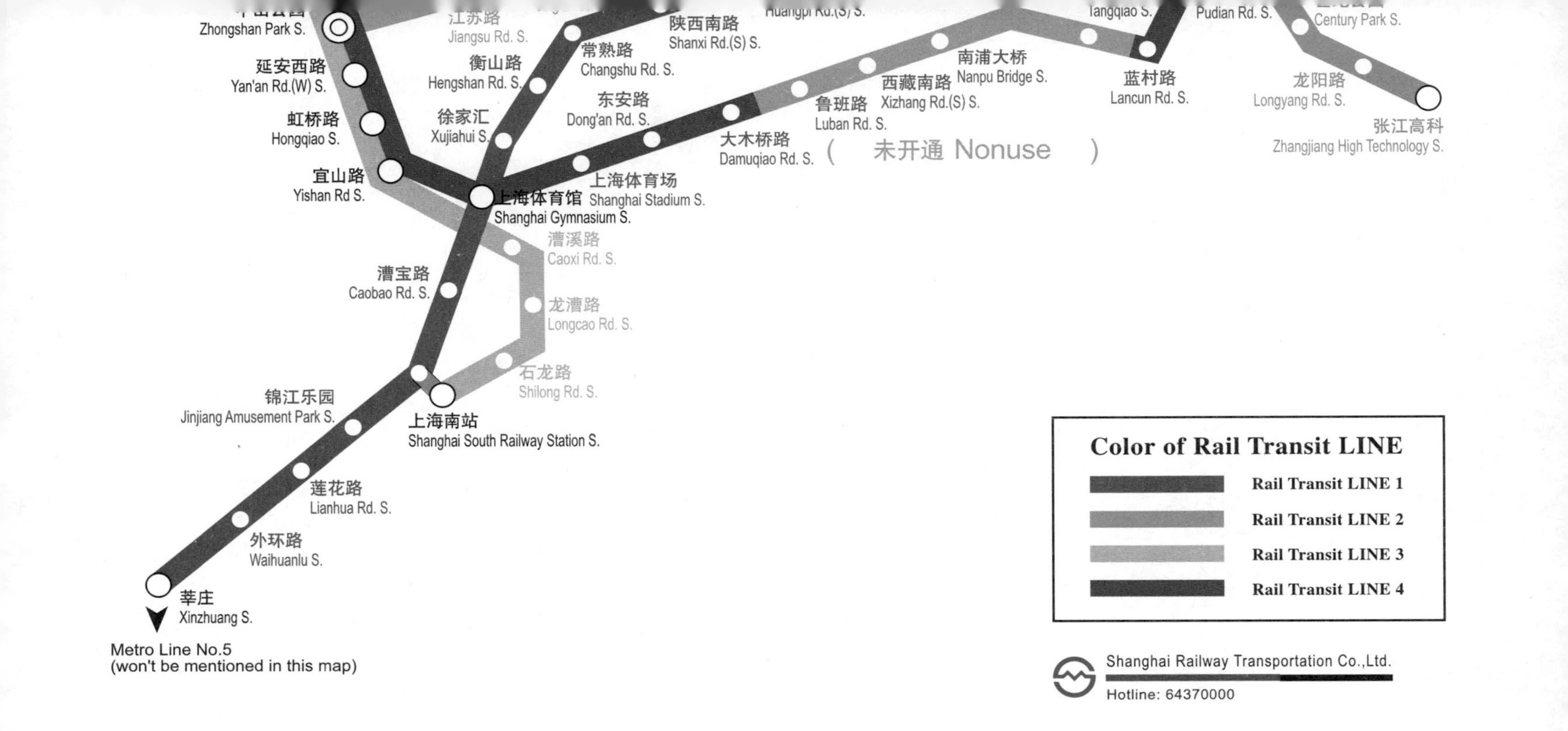

Zhongshan Park S.
延安西路
Yan'an Rd.(W) S.
虹桥路
Hongqiao S.
宜山路
Yishan Rd S.
江苏路
Jiangsu Rd. S.
衡山路
Hengshan Rd. S.
徐家汇
Xujiahui S.
常熟路
Changshu Rd. S.
陕西南路
Shanxi Rd.(S) S.
东安路
Dong'an Rd. S.
上海体育场
Shanghai Stadium S.
上海体育馆
Shanghai Gymnasium S.
大木桥路
Damuqiao Rd. S.
鲁班路
Luban Rd. S.
西藏南路
Xizhang Rd.(S) S.
南浦大桥
Nanpu Bridge S.
蓝村路
Lancun Rd. S.
Pudian Rd. S.
Century Park S.
龙阳路
Longyang Rd. S.
张江高科
Zhangjiang High Technology S.
(未开通 Nonuse)
漕溪路
Caoxi Rd. S.
龙漕路
Longcao Rd. S.
石龙路
Shilong Rd. S.
漕宝路
Caobao Rd. S.
上海南站
Shanghai South Railway Station S.
锦江乐园
Jinjiang Amusement Park S.
莲花路
Lianhua Rd. S.
外环路
Waihuanlu S.
莘庄
Xinzhuang S.

Metro Line No.5
(won't be mentioned in this map)

Color of Rail Transit LINE

Rail Transit LINE 1
Rail Transit LINE 2
Rail Transit LINE 3
Rail Transit LINE 4

Shanghai Railway Transportation Co.,Ltd.
Hotline: 64370000

Festivals and Custom

节庆与习俗

Spring Festival

Spring Festival come at the first day of the first lunar month every year, and is also called the lunar new year. It is the most ceremonious and lively traditional festival in China. Dating back to the ceremony to offer sacrifice to ancestors and gods in Yin and Shang period, it enjoys a long history.

Spring Festival custom

In this most important festival all the year round, there are many set customs on that day, such as spring cleaning, paste couplets and paper cuts, and the Chinese character of "fortune" up side down; New Year picture, staying up all night on New Year's Eve, firecrackers, paying a New Year visit, special food (new year cake and dumpling), etc.

Lantern Festival

It comes on the 15th day of the 1st lunar month. According to the traditional custom, people will light colorful lanterns to celebrate this moon night. The activities are admiring the moon, eating yuanxiao, get-together, etc.

Eating yuanxiao is a custom. And in many places some activities are added, such as playing dragon lantern and lion, walking on stilts, etc. This festival which has a history over 2,000 years is not only popular in mainland China, Taiwan, Hongkong, but also in overseas Chinese inhabited districts.

Lantern Festival Custom

Eating yuanxiao, admiring lanterns, getting rid of disease, etc. It is the Chinese Valentine's Day.

Mid-autumn Day

It happens on the 15th day of the 8th month on the lunar calendar. It is another festival for family get-together.

On that day, people will hold a banquet to admire the moon and wish their relatives and friends far way healthy and happy.

There are many customs on Mid-autumn Day representing people's love of life and hope of future.

Mid-autumn Day Custom

Admiring the moon and eating mooncakes are two major activities.

Tomb-Sweeping Day

A traditional Chinese festival, it is the most important day for offering sacrifice to ancestors and paying tribute to the dead. The Han people and some minor ethic sweep graves on Tomb-Sweeping Day.

Tomb-Sweeping Day Custom

The custom on Tomb-Sweeping Day is rich and interesting, like swing, football, spring outing, tree planting and kite flying, sweeping grave etc. Fire is prohibited.

Dragon Boat Festival

It happens on the 5th day of 5th month on the lunar calendar and is one of the oldest traditional Chinese festivals. Activities include: the married daughter visit her parents, hanging Zhongkui portrait, welcoming ghost boat, dragon boat racing, swing, covering the children with realgar, etc. People enjoy realgar liquor, calamus liquor, five poison cake, salt egg, zongzi and fresh fruits.

The Dragon Boat Festival was said to commemorate Quyuan. This is a mainstream legend, and spreads wide among commoners. The dragon boat racing and zongzi are all associated with Quyuan.

Telephone most commonly used

Inquiry about local telephone number	114	Time-inquiry	117
Inquiry about overseas long distance call	106	Inquiry about post code	184
Police	110	EMS	185
Fire	119	Railway info hot line	021-63179090
Ambulance	120	Hongqiao Int'l Airport aviation service	021-62688918
Weather	12121	Pudong Int'l Airport aviation service	021-96081388

Taxi

Qiangsheng Taxi Company
Tel: 021-62580000
Complain Tel: 021-62581234

Dazhong Taxi Company
Add: 1515 Zhongshan Rd (W)
Tel: 021-96822
Complain Tel: 021-173350

Bashi Taxi Company
Tel: 021-96840
Complain Tel: 021-62581234

Jinjiang Tour Taxi Company
Tel: 021-96961
Complain Tel: 021-64648888

Tourism Inquiry Service and Tourism Administration and Supervision Institutions

Shanghai Tourism Inquiry Service Center

Shanghai Tourism Inquiry Service Center
Add: Rm. 4014, No. 2525 Zhongshan Rd. (W)
Tel: 021-64397170

Jing'an District Tourist Information & Service Center
Add: No. 1612 Nanjing Rd. (W)
Tel: 021-62158703

Huangpu District Tourism Inquiry Service Center
Add: No. 561 Nanjing Rd. (E)
Tel: 021-53531118

Luwan District Tourism Inquiry Service Center
Add: No. 127 Chengdu Rd. (S)
Tel: 021-63728330

Chongming county Tourism Inquiry Service Center
Add: No. 60 Bayi Rd., Chengqiao
Tel: 021-59625888

Pudong New Area Tourism Inquiry Service Center
Add: No. 541 Dongfang Rd.
Tel: 021-68750593

Nanshi District Tourism Inquiry Service Center
Add: No. 159 Old Jiaochang Rd.
Tel: 021-63555033

Putuo District Tourism Inquiry Service Center
Add: No. 457 Changshou Rd.
Tel: 021-62980190

Zhabei District Tourism Inquiry Service Center
Add: No. 296-298 Tianmu Rd. (W)
Tel: 021-63538613

Songjiang District Tourism Inquiry Service Center
Add: No. 77 Zhongshan Rd. (M)
Tel: 021-57713745

Xuhui District Tourism Inquiry Service Center
Add: in Longhua Tourist City
Tel: 021-54104694

Railway Tourism Inquiry Service Center
Add: No.1 South Exit
Tel: 021-63539920

Shanghai Government and Related Association

Shanghai Municipal Tourism Administrative Commission
Tel: 021-64391818

Foreign Affairs Office of the Shanghai Municipal People's Government
Tel: 021-62565900

Office of Overseas Chinese Affaires of the Shanghai Municipal People's Government
Tel: 021-62490880

Office of Taiwan Affairs of the Shanghai Municipal People's Government
Tel: 021-62758877

Division fo Aliens & Exit Entry Adiministration of the Shanghai Municipal Public Security Bureau
Tel: 021-63576666

Shanghai Tourism Association
Tel: 021-64862853

Tourism Complaints

Shanghai Tourism Quality Supervision Office
Tel: 021-64393615

CAAC East China Administration
Tel: 62688899

Shanghai Harbour Passenger Transport Service Corporation
Tel: 021-65460730

Shanghai Railway Administration
Tel: 021-51225114

Shanghai Taxi Administration Department
Tel: 021-63232150

图书在版编目（CIP）数据

上海旅游实用指南. 英文／上海市旅游事业管理委员会，上海人民美术出版社编. －上海：上海人民美术出版社，2006.8

ISBN 7-5322-4778-3

Ⅰ.上. . . Ⅱ.①上. . . ②上. . . Ⅲ.旅游指南－上海市－英文 Ⅳ.K928.951

中国版本图书馆 CIP 数据核字（2006）第 025981 号

上海旅游实用指南

编　　者：上海市旅游事业管理委员会
　　　　　上海人民美术出版社

责任编辑：雨　鹰

助理编辑：周　艳

英文翻译：陈　春

英文审校：费玉英

封面设计：青　子

装帧设计：霍小旦

排　　版：及事文化传播

技术编辑：陆尧春

出版发行：上海人民美術出版社
　　　　　（上海长乐路 672 弄 33 号）

印　　刷：上海市印刷十厂有限公司

开　　本：787×1092　1/24　6 印张

版　　次：2006 年 8 月第 1 版

印　　次：2006 年 8 月第 1 次

印　　数：0001-5250

书　　号：ISBN 7-5322-4778-3/K·84

定　　价：48.00 元